CW01175462

No part of this publication may be reproduced, stored in a retrieval system, or transmitted in any form or by any means, electronic, mechanical, photocopying, recording, scanning, or otherwise, without the prior written permission of the publisher, except in the case of brief quotations within critical reviews and otherwise as permitted by copyright law.

NOTE: This is a work of fiction. Names, characters, places, and incidents are a product of the author's imagination. Any resemblance to real life is purely coincidental. All characters in this story are 18 or older.

Copyright © 2022, Willow Winters Publishing. All rights reserved

Zander & Ella

W. Winters & Amelia Wilde
Wall street journal & usa today bestselling authors

Playlist

Airplanes - B.o.B. featuring Hayley Williams

Ho Hey - The Lumineers

I Wanna Be Your Slave - Måneskin

Nothing More - Here's to the Heartache

Riptide - Vance Joy

AJR - Bang!

Pumped Up Kicks - Foster The People

I Love It - Icona Pop featuring Charli XCX

What Ifs - Kane Brown featuring Lauren Alaina

Somethin' Bad - Miranda Lambert and Carrie Underwood

From *USA Today* best-selling authors W Winters and Amelia Wilde comes a sinful romance with a touch of dark and angst that will keep you gripping the edge of your seat ... and begging for more.

He was mine. My protector, my lover.
My second start at life.
The man who promised me there was more than this.
He gave me hope.
Until my world fell apart again.
It was bound to happen. It's all life has given me.

Maybe he won't break his promises.
Maybe my heart won't shatter.
All I want ... is for love to be enough.

This is book 3 of the Love the Way You series. *Kiss Me* (book 1) and *Hold Me* (book 2) must be read first.

Love Me

Prologue

Ella

Four years ago, before tragedy struck

"You know I care for you, don't you?" he questions and there's a hint of something I can't place. Something in his tone he's never given me before. We've been on again and off again for years now. Something tonight is different.

"Of course I do." During all that's happened, he's always cared for me. God knows I've been to hell and back with a bottle of tequila, and he's been there all through the night and in the morning. He's cared in other ways too. Ones that give me this insecure feeling I can't shake. The wind blusters in, shifting the curtains and the moonlight stirs in the expansive room. There were boundaries before tonight, boundaries that seem to disappear when he looks at me like that.

James is the only lover I've ever had who's kept my secrets ... he's the only one I've told the darkest ones to.

"Then why won't you talk to me?" he asks.

As a chill sweeps along my shoulders, I pull the covers up higher, settling deeper into the bed.

"I think I love you," I tell him, although I'm reluctant to admit it. I roll onto my side as I do, pulling the satin sheets with me and ignoring the groan of the bed. I'm still sore between my thighs and I have to hold back a sated moan of content. The fan revolves in the silence and I turn from looking at the shadows it casts on the ceiling to stare at the man who's making me remember too much, making me feel too much.

James ... my on-again, off-again lover I can't resist.

His lips quirk up into a cocky smirk as he props himself up on one elbow and then moves a hand beside me, so that he towers slightly over me. Still silent, not giving an inch and only finding amusement in my statement.

A humorless laugh leaves me, and I press against his chest but he doesn't move. He continues staring down at me, watching and waiting. For what? I don't know.

"Leave me be, you sex fiend," I tease. "Sleep is tempting me and I'd like to take it up on its offer if I can." He knows how hard it is for me to sleep. Insomnia is something that bonded us. Oddly, with him in my bed, I sleep so much better. Rolling onto my side I pretend to ignore him and he lies down beside me, then nips the lobe of my ear, making me squeal. I can't help that the slight pain sends a ripple of want through me, reviving the pleasure I felt only moments ago.

"You think you love me?" he questions with a hint of awe in his tone and I'm forced to look at him over my shoulder.

It's hard to tell if he's toying with me. If he's playing around like we do with each other or if he's being serious.

"I have feelings for you," I whisper back, unwilling to be open and vulnerable until he is first. For some reason, when I look at him, refusing to give him what he wants, my chest aches. There's a tenderness for him I haven't felt before.

"Tell me you love me," he commands and my bottom lip drops, my body already wanting to give him anything he demands. It's dangerous, though. Especially for a girl like me. Kamden's warning is there on the tip of my tongue. Money is a drug that people will do anything and everything to obtain, and it can leave you with nothing. Love doesn't change that and my name alone is worth enough money that no one outside of my inner circle can ever be fully trusted. But Kamden knows James, and he knows what James knows.

That chill comes back again.

James's eyebrow cocks humorously. If he knew the thoughts racing in my mind, he wouldn't think it was so funny.

My expression slips before I can stop it and he moves to hover over me. "What's wrong?"

Pushing away from him, I wish he would stop. I wish it would all stop. "I don't want this life anymore. I don't—"

"El, I can give you whatever you want."

"Promises, promises," I whisper with my eyes closed, not wanting to think.

"I can promise you the world," he says with such sincerity my throat closes. They're the same promises my father gave my mother. The assurances that fool women into trusting men and leaning on them, into loving with everything they have. It's all too much.

"I don't need you to promise me the world, James," I tell him as if he needs reminding.

I smirk at him, and the spaghetti strap of my black silk cami falls down my shoulder. James's gaze follows it and there's a hunger there, a lust ... but when he looks back up at me, it shifts.

My heartbeat pauses, frozen where it is. As if it too wants to know if that's love in his gorgeous eyes.

"You don't need promises," he scoffs at me before kissing the tender spot on my neck. Whispering at the shell of my ear he says, "You love it when I fuck you like I did tonight, though, don't you?"

I can only hum in response, my body instantly responding to his as his warmth covers me. "You know why I love fucking you like I do?"

"Hmm?" is my only answer to him, as if I don't care, as if it's not a thought that keeps me up at night. He doesn't answer until my eyes are on him.

"I love that I tame you."

They say he fucks the wild out of me. He has me on a leash. I don't know how or why, but he does.

"You're saying love an awful lot tonight," I murmur.

"Is that really why you're acting differently? Because you love me?"

"Because I'm scared to love you." Before he can respond I add, "To love anyone."

"You can love me, Ella. I promise," he tells me. "I'll protect you, provide for you."

My gaze drops to the moonlight spilling across the bedroom floor. I can't look at him as the memories flash through my mind.

Promises, promises. Men give them out like candy. James whispers promises just like my father did to my mother.

Those promises he gave her that she fell for.

The promises he told before he killed her. And before I killed him.

Chapter 1

Zander

PRESENT TIME

The mixture of anger and fear are so intense that I could never calm myself. It's impossible to feel anything other than rage as my hands tremble. My feelings won't make any difference in the end, though. I'm going to do what I need to for Ella even if my heart is pounding so hard it threatens to leave my chest.

It hasn't stopped since I left the motel. This unwanted concoction of emotions threatens to consume me.

All I need to do is gain control over this situation. And that means getting to Ella. The sound of my footsteps echoing on the staircase is foreboding as I climb up to the next floor. My ears burn knowing everyone else knew where she was before me. The fact she called Kam over me is something I'll have to deal with later.

Speak of the fucking devil.

As I round the corner to the hall, Kam stands outside the door to her bedroom, his arms crossed over his chest. His irritation darkens his eyes and furrows his brow. The closer I get, the more palpable his anger is.

I'm thankful now for all the years on the job. Difficult clients and high-stress situations. High-risk scenarios. Nothing has ever felt like this before, though. Like I'm on the cusp of losing her. Losing everything. All my experience with The Firm means nothing if I don't have Ella. Kam can be pissed all he wants; he can't make me feel any worse than I do right now.

Kam draws himself up to his full height as I stop in front of him, the wooden floor creaking slightly. "You have no idea how badly you fucked up, do you?"

He squares up with me like he wants to fight and as much as I'd love to oblige, my feelings on the matter are irrelevant. Still, I sure as hell don't want to get into a discussion of whether or not I fucked up, let alone how it all happened. I want to get to Ella. I *need* to get to her. I will make damn sure she never runs from me again.

If Kam weren't her conservator, I'd ignore him entirely. As it is, she called him. I can't ignore that.

"Is she okay?" I ask in as level a tone I can manage, bypassing Kam's question to discuss the only topic that matters.

Kam lets out a breath. He's obviously pissed, but wary as well. His expression slips, revealing he's more scared than anything. Fuck. I didn't think I could sink any lower, that I could feel fear any more than I did the entire drive here.

"Is she all right?" I demand.

"Right now? She'll be okay," he admits finally. "I ran her a bath. When she's finished in there, she needs to get some sleep."

I can breathe again with a hint of relief. But only a hint. He continues, "Damon checked her out, and there's nothing wrong, but she needs rest. I was just stepping out to get her some water. She's ... not sober. I'll stay with her tonight."

"I'll be staying with her tonight."

"Zander, no. I—"

With my shoulder to him, I go around Kamden toward her bedroom. It's a good five feet away and I eat up the distance with him trailing behind me.

I half expect Kam to argue with me. He could try to drag me away from Ella's room, and I wouldn't put it past him. If I were in his shoes, I'd be doing the same. Both of us are trying to beat the other one to be the first to the door.

It doesn't really matter who's first. I'm going to go in. *She's mine.* This problem is mine to fix.

As we take the final steps to reach Ella, the fear comes back. I'll never be able to get those images of her out of my mind. The way she seemed to get more and more distant as the night went on. The panic I felt when she fell from that ledge. Leaving me in the middle of the night in a strange motel.

Something I did triggered her and led to her spiral. I saw it happening and I hung back thinking I could catch her at any moment. I failed her.

A cold sweat lingers on the back of my neck as I grip the glass doorknob.

I'm genuinely afraid to lose her, yet we've been reckless. I regret that. I should have been more careful with her. I also should have made a few things much clearer. I'll be rectifying that immediately.

That's the danger of falling in love. You break rules. Find excuses to justify your actions. She has clouded my judgment from the first moment I saw her. I knew better from the very beginning with Ella, but I couldn't stop myself. I felt too much for her.

In my own weakness, I risked losing her because I didn't have the strength to tear myself away. Now it's too late for that, even if Kam made a real attempt to stop me.

There is nothing that will keep me from her ever again.

Kam grabs my shoulder and turns me to face him. His expression is dead serious, the anger in his pale blue eyes cold and menacing.

"Listen," he says in a low voice, nearly a hiss, his hand still gripping my shoulder. "If you don't take control of this situation, then I will." His eyes search mine, his lips pressed in a grim line.

This isn't like him, but Kam's been pushed to the limit tonight. I see my own fear reflected in his eyes. He grits his teeth and continues. "Nothing that happened tonight can ever happen again. If you fail her, I'll destroy you."

The strength of conviction in his tone only makes me like the man more.

I can respect the protectiveness Kam feels right now, even if I think it should be solely my responsibility to care for her.

He could never take me from her, though. Not unless he killed me.

My first priority is Ella. It will be for as long as I'm alive. "Understood," I tell Kam. My tone isn't as even as I wanted. The tension in the air thickens. My muscles are ready for violence. It would at least take the edge off if we came to blows. Muffled sounds of Ella moving around inside her bedroom can be heard. She must be finished with her bath.

If we're going to fight, it'll have to be later. Kam seems to realize that at the same time I do. "Good."

He releases me and I release the knob, opting to knock on the door first. "Ella?"

There's no answer from the other side. I do a set of four-count breaths to calm the fuck down and focus, followed by another one. Then I open the door.

My heart races again the moment I cross the threshold. All of the terror that had been dampened from going toe to toe with Kam comes back full force.

Ella's sadness hangs in the air inside her bedroom. The space is clean, containing muted tones and decorated with expensive furniture. The mood isn't a neat and tidy one, though. It's heavy. Pervasive. Almost as if it's hard to breathe.

Ella leans against her dresser; the mirror is still one made of polished metal rather than glass. It's a reminder of what happened to her before.

With damp hair clinging to her back, she turns her head to look over her shoulder at me. Those beautiful chestnut eyes reach mine and there's longing there but something else too.

The sight of her makes my breath hitch. Wrapped only in a towel, her face is flushed from crying. Her cheeks are tearstained and her eyes rimmed in red. She's the epitome of sadness, and appearing so small in the expansive room, it only emphasizes how alone she must feel. Ella's home is beautiful, but it doesn't change the heartbreak in the woman standing in front of me.

Relief hits me harder, shocking my heart. There she is. She's alive, her heart still beating. She's still my Ella.

"Go away, Z." Her voice shakes as she tells me to leave. The sorrow shifts to something else as I close the door behind me. It shuts with a foreboding click.

I take a step toward her. And then another. All the while she stares at me, not daring to command me to do a damn thing.

With every step, a piece of me returns that she desperately needs. It's for her. Every fucking thing I do is for her.

Ella clutches the towel tighter to her chest. I take another step, reaching out a hand until my fingertips meet her skin.

Her strength begins to crumple at my touch. Ella's shoulders curve toward me, and I fold her into my arms. This is all I wanted when Kam was blocking my way in the hall. Ella in my arms where she belongs.

Cold droplets from her hair soak through my shirt, but her warm body molds to mine. She leans into me, letting me hold her. I can't help but kiss her temple, telling her in as soothing of a voice as I can, "That's better."

"Z, what are you doing here?" she questions, her face

still pressed to my chest.

"Did you think I wasn't going to come?"

She pulls away slightly, enough to look up at me and whispers, "It might be better if you go."

"Who am I to you?" My voice is harder now, and it's exactly what she needs.

Ella's breathing grows ragged as her eyes shine with new tears. I knew she'd be afraid. I knew she'd question whether I was going to come for her. It's what caused her to melt down at the party. Her uncertainty is something I have to be patient with. Something I need to tame.

"Who am I to you?" I ask again.

Ella's expression falls. "You should go—"

"Ella, answer me. Who am I to you?"

I emphasize each word, leaning closer. The heat between us is intense enough to burn my skin. She takes a rough breath but doesn't answer.

Ella's shoulders tremble. It's a sign her walls are coming down. It's what I'm waiting for. I'm not going to back off until she's okay.

Sadness, hurt and guilt coat the back of my throat. I did wrong by Ella. I should have stopped her or stopped myself. I should never have let us reach the point where she felt like this.

I know now. And I will fix this. If it's the last fucking thing I ever do, I will fix this.

She meets my eyes, and Ella's softening now. Giving in.

"Z," she says softly. Her heart is broken. I can hear it in her voice.

"Who am I to you?"

"My Dom."

"That's right. Act like it." She stiffens.

My heart pounds viciously as I gentle my tone to add, "I'm sorry."

Her eyes widen as we stand in our embrace. "I should have caught you and stopped you from running. I should have been stricter and transparent at the party," I say, lifting her chin with my forefinger, forcing her to look at me when she attempts to look away.

"Tonight was my fault, but you shouldn't have run and you better not push me away."

She swallows thickly.

"Who am I to you?" I ask for the final time, running my hands down her shoulders in a soothing motion. She's fragile right now. Far too fragile to punish how I'd like.

More tears glisten in her eyes, and she releases a heavy breath. The horrible distance I felt when I came into the room fades. I'm relieved as all hell. I couldn't have lived with myself if Ella put up more walls or, God forbid, ran away from me again. I've survived plenty of things, but that's the limit.

"You're my Dom," Ella says confidently and calmly.

Those words out of her mouth are all I need to know it'll be okay. At least for tonight.

"Are you done, jailbird?"

Ella steels herself. "You ... you should probably go. I don't want you to see me like this."

"It's my wants you should concern yourself with. Let go of every other thought. I want you right now. Fuck, no. I need you right now. I'm not leaving, and neither are you." The confidence comes easy now. We're in the roles we're meant to play. I'm her Dom, and she's not going to send me away. "You're going to get into that bed, and I'm going to hold you until you close your eyes. You're going to sleep off the alcohol and every other messed-up thought you just had. And when you wake up, and I make sure you're all right—"

"Z," she says, her voice nearly breaking into a whimper.

"After that." I lower my voice and pull her face close to mine. I want my jailbird to hear every word. She might not be certain of us right now. She might be too shaken to realize that I'm never leaving. But for tonight, she's going to know exactly what's coming next. "You're going to pay for what you just did, Ella."

She makes a soft sound.

"Your ass is going to feel that punishment. Your cunt. Your mouth. I'm going to claim every inch of you until there isn't a single thought in that pretty little head of yours other than that you belong to me."

With a hand over hers and the other on the small of her back, I lead her to the bed, gently but demanding. "Under the covers," I tell her, pulling back the sheets.

She doesn't hesitate to get into bed, but she doesn't lie down. Instead she pulls the sheet to her chest and peers up at me with wide eyes brimming with emotion. "Will you stay with me until I fall asleep?"

"The fact that you asked me that tells me I haven't done the job I need to." I didn't think it was possible to feel such a drift from her. She's pulled away, but I'll pull her right back and hold on to her forever.

Pulling my shirt over my head, I tell her to lie down. I kick off my shoes and strip down to my boxers before climbing into bed, pulling her back into my chest and kissing her hair. It only takes a few minutes before her shoulders tremble and I know she's crying.

I soothe her and hold her, rubbing her back and kissing her over and over.

"I'm sorry," she whispers and I tell her it's all right. She has nothing to be sorry for. I do, though. I'm sorrier than she could ever imagine.

Chapter 2

Ella

Everything is different this morning. It's like the fog has cleared and now each destructive thought and the resulting consequences are highly visible. It's hard to describe this unsettled feeling, but the way I'd put it is that if the barred door to my gilded cage were wide open, I wouldn't move an inch from where I sit. Not because I don't crave freedom, but because I'm terrified of what I'd do with it.

The wind carries a slight chill that whisks across my arms and I'm quick to pull the gray crocheted throw blanket up around myself more. I breathe in the brisk woodsy air and sink back into the porch chair.

I wouldn't move an inch and I don't have to. It's

something Kam has always reassured me of. I'm okay here and I can stay safely inside for however long I want; the door is always open and he'll be there to hold my hand if needed. Inside or outside.

He was there for me before. And then there was James.

The thought tightens a vise that's soldered to my heart. Zander is only feet away inside the house, more than likely watching the session. And yet here I am, reminded of what once was. The past that he'll never fully know because I'm incapable of speaking of it.

"Your voice sounds much better than it did only weeks ago," Damon comments. His teacup is empty but he keeps picking it up as if he's going to take a sip from it.

Absently, the tips of my fingers graze my throat as I watch him. I wonder if it's a sign of anxiousness on Damon's part. I've never seen him fidget like that before, repeatedly lifting the empty cup and setting it down.

Even through the heavier conversations, he's usually still or taking notes. Today has been relatively quiet so far and as the teacup clinks against the saucer, I imagine he has something he'd like to discuss but doesn't know how to start.

"My throat feels better," I comment idly. "It feels a lot better actually." Everything is better, depending on how you look at it.

My gaze shifts to my left, peeking over my shoulder to

the living room where Zander may be sitting. The thick curtains are mostly drawn shut and looking through the tiny slit in the middle I can tell Zander's not there. The leather chair is empty.

Nervousness pricks through me.

"Is there anything you'd like to discuss today, Ella?" Damon presses as he lifts one ankle over his knee and sits back in his chair as if it's a casual conversation.

He knows what happened. That I drank too much, I made a fool of myself ... I had a moment.

Dread comes over me. I don't want to talk about it.

James and Zander compete in the back of my mind but they both tell me I have to talk about it. The knowledge chills me as if James is here, as if he wants Z to command me to say the words out loud. I have to get everything out of me or it will kill me.

That's one thing I imagine they'd both agree on. It's going to eat me alive.

"Can we talk about James?" Damon says, moving the conversation forward and all I do is nod, staring off into the distance.

"I didn't know love until James." My statement is a murmur, but Damon hears it. His pen clicks and I glance to see his pad open.

"Why do you say that?" he questions, his dark eyes on me holding nothing but compassion.

"My mother used me as a bargaining chip, my father did the same when I was old enough … the things he made me do I'll never forget or forgive." Glancing down I find I'm picking at my nails. Readjusting myself in the seat, I get more comfortable and pull the throw blanket up again. Practically hiding under it although my head remains poking out.

"He was your first boyfriend or—"

"No," I answer honestly and I'm certain Damon is already aware. "Every lover was only a partner for sex. There's no family to speak of other than my mother and father." Trish and Kam and Kelly flick across my memory at the mention of family.

Damon comments as if reading my mind, "You had your friends, though. You've been close with them for longer than you were with James, haven't you?"

"Yes. Yes, and I love them. It's just a different love."

Damon nods thoughtfully. "Well, that makes sense."

I do love my friends; they know this game as well as I do. The lies and the depths to which others will go. And they've been there for me as I was for them. There was that … partnership, that dependency …

But then there was James.

And now … Zander is bringing up things he shouldn't. He's making me feel things he shouldn't. I don't know how to simply turn it off.

"Do you want to tell me what happened?" Damon presses.

"I had a drink and I shouldn't have," I answer mildly, picking at the throw.

"It's me, Ella. You can talk to me."

"What if I don't want to talk?" I'm surprised by how blunt my answer is. He's only trying to help and I'm more than aware of that. A part of me desperately wishes to tell him everything. But I don't understand it. I don't know why I can't turn it off.

"You don't have to talk to me, but you may want to when I'm not here and I'm here now. I'm worried, Ella," Damon tells me and that anxiousness shines through. His teacup sits unattended on the table. It's his tone that gave it away.

"I'm worried too," I answer him and my throat goes tight. This time it's me reaching for my cup and finding it empty.

"Grief is a ball in a box ... is love like that too?"

"What do you mean?" he asks and his head tilts. For such a strong and dominating man, Damon has a tenderness about him. A thoughtful caring that coaxes out the conversation I want to keep buried inside. The one I'm not ready to have.

"I remember how much I love him, or loved," I answer softly and then swallow thickly.

He's gentle, but quick to answer, "You never stop loving someone. You can use it in present tense."

Tears prick my eyes and I dab the corners of them as if they don't fall recklessly at the memory of James.

I will always love him, but I love Zander ... And dare I say I love him more?

Sniffling, I ignore the fact that the trickle of tears turns to sobs. My hand shakes too hard to gently dab so I bring my chin to my knees and press the throw blanket to my eyes instead.

"I'm not okay," I admit to Damon.

"You may think you aren't, but I'm looking at you and I know this is okay. I know you are going to get through this. Are you thinking things that aren't okay? Ella, are you thinking about hurting yourself?"

Shaking my head I say, "I just miss him." At the admission, surprise courses through me enough that the tears stop. I'm not thinking of that at all. When everything first happened, I was plagued with thoughts of driving down the highway and plummeting off a bridge. Or taking a long hot bath and drawing a knife down my wrists. Those ideas are what got me sent away to the Rockford Center, because I truly thought of suicide almost every waking hour. Just ending it.

"I don't want to kill myself," I tell Damon.

"Did you last night?"

"No." My answer is easy and spoken only in a breath. "I was shocked and worried because I felt the loss all over again, but I didn't want that."

"When's the last time you've had those thoughts?" he asks.

"Since before ... since I was in Rockford."

"I just want to be very clear and make sure I understand. Are you thinking anything that would be alarming? This is a safe place, Ella. We won't make you go back or do anything outside of your comfort zone. Know that before answering this question. Are you thinking about hurting yourself at all or in any way?"

"No. But I'm thinking I wish I was with him."

And that makes me feel like I'm cheating on Zander. Like I'm a truly horrible person. He deserves so much more and so much better than a woman who misses her first love. Who will always miss him.

"He shouldn't want me." Not when I'm so thoroughly broken by what happened with James. "Zander shouldn't want me." James said he would ruin me and I swear he did. I love him. I do, but I love Zander more. Even if it makes me an awful person.

"I don't understand it and I'm scared."

"Scared of what?"

"Scared that I'm undeserving."

I love what he does to me, though. The control and

the heat that burns between us. Last night comes back in full force and I swear I can feel his warm breath in the crook of my neck. My eyes become heavy and desire along with something else floods into my blood. He feels that too. I'm able to give him that at the very least and I'm certain he enjoys it.

"He knows what he wants and he wants you as you are."

I stare back at Damon. "Has he told you that?"

He answers my question with one of his own. "Hasn't he told you that?"

"Has he told me ..." It takes a moment to put the pieces together. "Has Z told me he wants me?"

Damon nods and waits for me to answer.

"He has," I say and the admission is a whisper. "He makes it very clear what he wants." My heart thumps hard in my chest, painfully so. I've told him I love him and he hasn't said it back.

Maybe that's a good thing. My gaze drops and I grab a tissue, blowing my nose and getting over the sorrow I feel for myself when I'm the one causing so much pain for everyone else.

Chapter 3

Zander

I type out one last message to the group chat on my phone and send it: **I'll take care of it.**

End of discussion. She's had time to process. Spoken to Kam and Damon. Now it's my turn.

Cade and Damon have been texting nonstop in a whirlwind of discussion. They have their wants, their preferences, and their concerns.

But I'm the only one who knows what Ella requires. What she desperately needs and it's time that I give it to her and in return she'll give me every fucking worry she has.

I've heard all I need to hear from my brother and Damon and Kam. And Ella for that matter.

"Everything okay?" she questions. Her dark eyes are soulful and inquisitive. She is still shaken from the events of her breakdown, but surer of herself now.

"Of course, jailbird."

I take her hand in mine and lead her to the room down the hall. To a door that will lead her to punishment and pleasure. To a room where she can let it all go. And give it to me.

Ella looks at the closed door, her breathing shallow. I take a minute to step back and assess her. She is anxious, possibly from the thought of her punishment. Better than last night for sure. We can do this. This is the next step.

"Open the door, Ella," I tell her.

With a heavy inhale she obeys. Her eyes widen slightly and her chest rises with shock at the newly decorated room.

"It's different," she whispers with a touch of awe in her voice. A smirk gently lifts my lips, but it comes and goes before she can see it.

"I ... redecorated."

It's the BDSM room. A playroom. Silas helped move everything from my place to hers. We worked while she slept last night and put the finishing touches on while she had her session with Damon. I haven't slept at all, but this was needed.

My equipment has been arranged around the room. The air is cool, not too cold. The window lights the room from behind a thin curtain although I can pull the thick drapes shut if needed. I want her to see this, though. Every piece is placed with purpose. The traditional armoire with paddles and whips rests beside the padded bench. The horse has the addition of knee support, I imagine she's going to love that piece, given how much pleasure she gets when I take her from behind.

The scent is of freshly polished wood and leather. It's faint and not overbearing.

I watch her move around the space, fingertips reaching out to glide along the luxurious furniture. My heart races again at the memory that I almost lost her. My fear slips in with the anger, and I breathe it out. Never again. She will regret ever leaving me in a moment of chaos.

She turns to face me, hesitant, waiting. As if realizing her punishment is imminent.

"You are in need, Ella," I tell her. "And you will not stop me from providing you with what you need." Her breath hitches as a flush creeps into her cheeks. "Understood?"

"Yes, Z."

"Good ..." My gaze drifts to her silk nightgown and my cock twitches with desire. "Take off your clothes."

She does as I tell her. Her curves are quickly unveiled

as the silk slips into a puddle around her feet. Her lace bra and panties are next, joining the pale pink fabric on the floor. Then she faces me, hands clasped in front of her, her naked body beautiful before my eyes.

Heat floods through me. My hand flexes with the need to feel her skin redden beneath it.

"You had rules before," I state, my body already responding to hers. I'm hard and ready to take her. However, I'm not focused on myself in the slightest. All my attention is on her. "Today, you're mine, and from here on out, no other rules matter. Not the company's rules, not Kamden's rules. No formal rules except the ones we make right now. Even the fucking law is irrelevant. Is that understood?"

"Yes, sir," she says breathlessly as I round her, pacing and making certain she hears everything crystal clear.

"Give me your wrists." Ella offers them to me with sweet submission.

I take them in mine with one hand and lead her to the bed. With the fireplace crackling in the corner, she'll be warm here, but not too hot. Her body temperature, like everything else, is important to me. I don't want her to overheat. I also don't want her to shiver.

Nothing but pain and pleasure. Punishment and security.

"Lie down on the bed," I say, loosening my black silk

tie, leaving me in gray suit pants and a button-down that will both be on the floor in a matter of time.

Ella lies back on the bed, her body spread out before me, and I turn to my next task.

I tie her down slowly, like it's the most important thing I've ever done. It *is* the most important thing I've ever done. Each new moment with her becomes the most important. All of them will build on each other until she's whole again.

With her hands secured above her head, tied to the headboard, I put a spreader bar between her ankles. The clicks of the restraints resonate in the room. Fuck, she's gorgeous.

My jailbird is completely exposed to me now. She's completely vulnerable to me. Bound to the bed by my own hands. As I complete her bindings, I speak to her, adding one light kiss to her lips.

Otherwise, I don't touch her. Only necessary touches that leave goosebumps in their wake.

I won't touch her until we've discussed the rules and she acknowledges them and agrees. The kiss was the only exception.

"Rule number one, Ella." Her eyes come to mine as she waits silently. "You will not leave my side unless I agree to it. Ever."

I swallow thickly, knowing how extreme it is. Given

what occurred, it is a requirement from here on out.

A second passes, her eyes on mine. She listens, she hears it ... and ultimately, she agrees.

"Yes, sir." She's eager to please me. As a reward I slide my fingertips over her soft folds. Her back bows slightly and a soft murmur spills from her lips. She's ready, slick for me, but not as ready as she will be when I'm finished. I stroke her clit with my thumb. A few seconds. That's all. Reinforcing her obedience.

Her chest rises and falls with her heavy breaths. Standing beside the bed, I slowly unbutton my shirt. "What's rule number two?" she whispers.

I reach into the side table, taking out a butt plug and the small bottle beside it. Applying adequate lube, I warm it for her. "Rule number two. No alcohol again. Ever. Unless I give it to you."

Ella's friends say she doesn't have addiction issues. Damon agrees there's a difference between misuse and addiction. Right now, she's not allowed to use alcohol as a crutch, though. If she's triggered while inebriated ... she will spiral faster. I have to contain her.

The bed groans as I place my hand on it and lean to tower over her. I look deeply into Ella's eyes. "Is that understood?"

"Yes, sir," she answers without hesitation.

A moment passes as I move to the foot of the bed so

I can do as I please. I angle her hips slightly, lifting the spreader bar and twisting it enough to give me access to what I want, and push the plug gently inside her. Ella gasps a little, her hips rocking back and forth. I rub a small circle over her clit as her reward.

"That's my good girl," I tell her.

My praise and small touches have Ella close already. I can see that in the trembling of her muscles. Part of me wants to let her come, but I pull away. Her hooded eyes snap to mine.

"There were boundaries you and James had, correct?"

She blinks, seemingly startled by the question. Perhaps by the mention of James. I don't miss how the cords in her neck tighten as she swallows. "Yes," she replies slowly.

"What are they?"

"I'm not sure I can remember them all." She gives a small shake of her head as if she's reluctant to even try.

"You know some of them, which brings me to rule number three. When you discover another trigger, you will confide in me immediately. You will run to me. You will cry in my arms. You will break for me and me alone. I share your pleasure, jailbird, and that means I also share your pain. Is that understood?"

"Yes, sir," she answers.

"Can you remember some of those boundaries, Ella?"

"No talking about our families." She squirms uncomfortably on the bed.

I'm quick to rectify her discomfort, kissing along her curves. "Is there anything else?"

She shakes her head although I'm almost certain she'd prefer the pleasure. "Ella, what are the words you don't want me to say?"

"Wild. Don't call me wild or say anything like that. Or tame." The request flows beautifully from her lips, without hesitation.

"Anything else?" I question and then kiss her breast.

"No. Just ... that."

"What about mentioning James?" I ask.

She hesitates, thinking it over. "I want to tell you about him."

I smile against her lips before kissing her.

"That would make me very happy," I confide in her. "Thank you for being such a good girl for me."

I push my fingers into her. With even strokes she comes quickly. Ella clenches down on my fingers and cries out with her climax. Her moans are low and sweet as she struggles against her bindings. I keep her restrained with my knee pressed down on the spreader bar.

Ella's completely at my mercy. Her face is red and flushed, her hair a messy halo.

"You're so fucking gorgeous when you come," I

praise, my voice low.

"I'm going to blindfold you now," I tell her before flipping her over, maneuvering her delicate weight in my hands with the spreader bar. Ella yelps in surprise. Her wrists are crossed now. The restraints are tighter. I slide a pillow under her belly, angling her how I want, then get up, leaving her alone. Until I return with the blindfold, carefully tying it into place.

"Z?" she says, her voice trembling.

"I'm here," I reassure her.

I open the bottle of water left on the dresser, then open up a pill bottle next. The Viagra goes down with a sip. This session is going to last a long time, and I need to last with her.

"Repeat the three rules back to me," I say.

She takes a deep breath. "I don't leave your side unless you consent. I'll never drink again, unless you give me the drink. And ..."

"Keep going."

"And I'll tell you the moment I'm aware I'm triggered."

"What else, Ella?"

"You'll punish me however you see fit, for however long you want. Do I still have my safe word?"

"You'll always have your safe word."

I lean down and press a kiss to her lips. "Thank you," she whispers.

Desire makes me harder. "You know I care for you, don't you?"

Ella nods.

"Good. Remember that today, and tonight, while I fuck you like my personal whore."

With every detail laid out and agreed to, I climb on the bed and position myself. Precum leaks from my cock and I use it to stroke myself. Ella speaks again. "Z?"

"Yes?"

"Do you ... want me?" she questions.

I know what she's asking. Do I want her more than just a game? As more than just a Dom/sub relationship?

I more than want you, Ella. I love you.

The words are on the tip of my tongue, but Ella lifts her head and I lean down to kiss her lips, whispering to her that she should know just how much I want her. Every fucking moment of every day and night.

With my reassurance she rests her head against the pillow and I move beside Ella, readying myself for her punishment.

"You scared me, Ella. You left me alone and refused me."

Her breath comes in ragged pants now. "I'm sorry," she says.

"Twenty for that, my little jailbird. You'll count." I bring my palm down on her ass, over and over again. Each time I strike a different area, starting from her upper thigh and moving higher. She whimpers, biting down on her lower lip and cries out my name but doesn't protest.

Ella counts each one and I don't stop until her ass is red.

Then I move behind her and push my cock into her.

It takes everything in me not to come instantly as she pushes back, eager for that reprieve of stinging pain. "Please," she begs me and I lean forward, kissing her neck as I fuck her ruthlessly. This is the part that's fucking heaven.

I let her come twice before I move to her ass. I play with the plug, toying with her and listening to her moans. Her head thrashes from side to side and I know she's close.

I grab the small bottle of lube, letting the cool liquid drizzle down her heated skin before replacing the plug with my cock.

Ella shudders as I take her tight hole inch by inch. The sight of her biting down on her lip to quiet her moans is enough that I lose myself. Coming doesn't matter, though; I'm still hard as a rock for her. It's impossible to hold myself back. She belongs to me and being buried in her is all I've wanted all day.

Her body is tense as I rock into her. Slowly at first, letting her adjust until finally I take her fully and fuck her ass mercilessly.

Another orgasm hits her as I spill myself into her again. But I'm not finished.

Pulling out, I spank her again and again and again, making sure every inch of her ass is red, reminding her that she's mine. Squeezing her reddened skin, I heighten the pain-pleasure threshold and then fuck her again.

For hours. Enjoying her however I fucking want.

Chapter 4

Ella

"Have you been taking your medication, babe?" he asks me with one brow cocked and a smirk on his lips. The look he gives me is comical and it's one I've seen a thousand times.

I smirk back and say, "I have." My silk nightie rides up under the covers as I pull my knee up to rest my chin on it. He can't see a thing, but still, I tug it back into place and cock a brow in return as I tell him, "Medication and dick work wonders for a girl like me."

Kam's smirk widens to a grin and mine follows with a nonchalant shrug. Even that small movement reawakens the soreness between my thighs and I bite down on my lower lip to stifle the moan that begs to spill from me.

There's no polite way to say it: Z fucked the hell out of me.

And I loved every sordid minute of it. I haven't slept so well or felt this content in ... well, I don't dare to remember.

Kam plops down on the other side of the sofa from where I'm sitting in the living room and the sofa offers a groan in response.

My tea is the perfect temperature and as far as I know, Zander is still sleeping soundly. Silas and Damon are in the other room, giving me privacy in the early morning. It's all comfortable now.

As if everything has settled and all is as it should be for the moment.

"I think most of life's problems can be solved with a pill or dick," I half-heartedly joke and hope the comment hits as intended.

"Or money," Kam chimes in and I'm quick to agree.

He toys with the thin black tie he wears; he must've left his jacket in the foyer. Without it Kam looks so much younger, yet the wrinkles around his eyes seem to have worsened. The last year has aged him immensely.

My gaze drops and apparently Kam sees it as his cue to pipe up. "So ... how are you really?"

Chewing the inside of my cheek, I pause only a

moment before I answer honestly, letting the truth slip out easier than it has recently. "I feel guilty ... moving on—" A chill drenches me as I admit it.

Kam's head shakes immediately as he cuts me off. "First, no guilt allowed. And second, you aren't moving on."

My throat tightens and I shake off the prickling sensation that runs down my arms.

"James would want you to be loved thoroughly ... and quite often," he jokes and it lightens the mood.

With a short huff of a laugh, I nod but it doesn't stop the bits of pain I feel whenever I think about James.

"So don't feel guilty. Or I'll have to tell your...your... what do you call him? Boy toy?"

A genuine laugh bubbles out. "Z is my boy toy?" I question humorously.

"Well, what is he to you? Just your Dom? Or...?" he asks.

Heat blazes across my skin and a tension settles through me. I could see him being more. So much more. But just the idea is stifling.

"Or rather, what should I call him?" Kam shifts the question and then pats my leg as he readjusts to face me more directly. "I suppose I could always just call him Zander, and not complicate it?" he offers and I'm quick to agree, releasing every ounce of apprehension that threatens to overwhelm me.

Before I can verbalize my answer, Kam says, "So if you're feeling guilty, I'll have to tell Zander to fuck that out of you, or spank it or … whatever kink you two agree on." He gestures in the air with a comical expression on his face that soothes so much of what ails me.

"Sex … no guilt," I say, summing up the conversation.

"That's right."

"Got it."

"We've had this conversation before," I comment and remember sitting on a sofa similar to this one a little over a year ago, promising I would stop feeling guilty, that I would stop thinking about all the dark things. It was just after the first time I tried to kill myself.

Kam had tears in his eyes then. They were raw and bloodshot. I'd never seen him like that.

"We have definitely had this conversation before." He nods in agreement and just as guilt starts to trickle in he says, "And it's okay to have it again. There's nothing wrong with that." He leans in closer, lowering his voice to jokingly add, "It would be great if it was the last time, but you can be a slow learner." I can't help the laugh. It's genuine and so out of place, but also so very needed.

A moment passes that settles everything. He lays his hand over mine and I flip mine over, so my palm is facing up and touching his. I give a gentle squeeze and he returns it.

His head falls back and he stares up at the ceiling. "Last time instead of guilt we were going to drink, but this time I think maybe instead of guilt"—with his head resting against the back of the sofa, he turns just slightly so his eyes are on mine to say—"we just have sex."

At my laugh he smiles, his pearly white teeth showing off how charming and handsome he is.

"Is that your way of telling me you've found a new boyfriend?"

"Ah, yes, I have a new boy toy."

"Really?" I shift to face him. A giddiness comes over me at the thought of Kam falling in love again, especially after things didn't work out with Gerald, his ex. If ever someone deserved a happily ever after, it's Kam. He's dedicated his life to our circle of friends and made whatever sacrifices were necessary. Ones we aren't supposed to mention. Some I wasn't meant to know of at all.

Just as I part my lips to ask who he is, he presses on about Zander.

"Let's talk about yours, though. About Zander."

"What about him?"

"The media reaction is exactly what we wanted and it also offers you a choice. Whichever you make, I'll support."

I pause, waiting for him to say it out loud although I can already guess what the options are.

"You can keep him or leave him. Our reaction determines what they perceive and given his position with The Firm, as well as legally ... there won't be any issues either way."

"Do we have to make any statement at all?" I question, thinking pragmatically. Silence is golden. That's my mantra and it's been my mantra for years.

"Not at all. It is good timing for public relations, though. The spotlight is on you, babe."

"Mm-hmm," I hum in understanding. Picking at my nails, I struggle to think of anything I want anyone to know. It's all too fresh and raw. I just want more time before I give them anything at all.

"If you want him to stay, he stays. If you want him to go ..." He gives a little wave, his hand making a rolling motion. I know what "go" means.

It's been ages since Kam last saw to a relationship ending. Prior to James. It's a final decision and one that can't be undone without extensive damage control.

"You can take time if you need," Kam starts. "I can keep him away if you want space to think—"

"I want him to stay." My statement is firm and Kam's lips lift in an asymmetric grin, giving me a sense of peace at my answer. Good. With that look I know everything will be all right.

It will be, won't it?

"I thought you'd say that. I thought you might tell me you love him." His gaze is locked with mine as he stares back at me expectantly. I can't answer, though. It seems more final to admit it to Kam than to Zander himself.

I can't do it. Not when I don't even know how Z really feels about me. Not when I don't know if this is going to last.

"Keep your secrets," he says, throwing his hands up with his lips pressed into a thin smile and then he breaks eye contact to look away. "You don't need to tell me anything more."

He readjusts on the sofa and I can only watch him until he looks back at me. Déjà vu comes over me and the theoretical clouds rumble in the distance.

"Just let me know if things change, all right?"

"Right. You'll be the first to know."

"And I'll take care of it."

He did the same for James. It's as if history is repeating itself. At that thought, chills run down my spine. I can barely swallow but before the intense emotion takes hold, Kam distracts me with an odd fact.

"Did you know that sex can occasionally result in transient global amnesia?" Kam tells me.

"What do you mean?"

"You can forget for a couple of hours."

"Forget what?" I question.

"Forget anything ... everything," he says jokingly and I have to smile as he gives me a grin.

It's quiet for a moment and I sink back, feeling as if I'm either in the eye of the storm, or the dark gray skies have passed and I'm just not aware of it yet.

After a moment, he breaks the silence.

"Your friends are worried about you," he tells me softly, patting the back of my hand and giving me a somewhat sad smile, but more like one with empathy.

"I'm worried about me too," I admit and consider jotting down some thoughts in the journal Damon gave me, the one with the rose gold binding. When Kam leaves, I think I'll do just that.

"It may sound odd, but that's a step up from last time." Kam nods as he speaks. "A good step," he adds, continuing the nodding. It's what he does when he's decided on a plan and is content with it. Those little nods provide so much comfort. More than he could ever realize. "You're worried, and I'll take that. Plus you're getting laid, so that's a good sign."

A huff leaves me. "It'll make me forget."

"Exactly."

"We have so much to forget, don't we?" My tone is slightly somber, which follows the path my mood drifts.

"Hmm..." he hums as if truly considering and I nearly laugh. "Not that I can remember," he jokes back.

Chapter 5

Zander

Seated across from Ella in the blue room, I can't help but come to the realization that's been following me since our last session.

It didn't just change things for her. It changed things for me. The way we were together unlocked something buried deep down. The fire crackles, keeping the expansive room warm even though the chill of late fall has set outside.

That one truth, that something has shifted inside of me, is something I've been keeping at bay with four-count breaths for months now.

I couldn't really admit it to myself.

But now, looking at Ella ...

I know.

Everything has changed and it can never go back to what it once was. It's not only that I want to share myself with her. It's that I'm finally ready to stop carrying the burden of these thoughts by myself. I've been attempting to give Ella some of the same relief about her own past. How can I do that when I won't do the same for myself? I know she feels this is one sided. Damon told me that she even claimed she was undeserving. It's because I haven't leaned on her as a Dom should. It works both ways. If anyone knows that, it's me.

It's hypocritical to not confide in her, and I don't want to be hypocritical with her. I want to be myself. And these thoughts, these ideas, are part of me.

It's only right to share them with her.

If Ella knew, then I wouldn't be the only one. I wouldn't have to carry it all by myself. It's time to let this go. The only way I can do that is by confiding in her.

"What are you thinking about?" Ella asks me from her place in the armchair across from mine. She's delectable this evening, in a cream silk slip designed just to taunt me. Her dark hair is swept over one shoulder, revealing her slender neck which carries a faint mark from last night as I nipped her in the heat of the moment. "Hmm?" she presses and her chestnut eyes pierce into me.

I want to deflect and move on to another topic.

That's been an old habit of mine. But I force myself not to do it.

"I was just thinking that I wanted to tell you something."

"Oh?" Her voice is even but her brow raises and there's a worrisome look that I don't like.

Smirking, I add, "It's like you could read my mind."

She huffs a small laugh at my comment.

"It's about Quincy," I warn her, testing her boundaries. She doesn't shift, she doesn't react in the least other than to nod, as if to tell me to continue.

"I think Quincy wanted me to tell her that I loved her," I admit, my throat feeling sore around the words.

"The night she died?" Ella's voice is soft and accepting.

I nod. "And before that, there were so many times she wanted me to say it. I knew she wanted that, and I never did." Deep regret pierces through me.

Ella glances out the window, looking thoughtful. My heart beats faster. "You'll tell me if you'd rather not discuss her."

"I want to." She's quick to quell any second thoughts about confiding in her. Moving from her seat of solitude, she comes to me. And I make room for her. Just this, her soft touch and warmth, is enough.

Nestled beside me, she looks back into my eyes. "Did you love her?"

There's no judgment in her tone. Only the desire for truth.

"Yes," I admit. "I did love her. Maybe not in the way she wanted and not in the way I craved from a partner, but I still loved her." I wrap my arm around her waist to tell her that it doesn't affect what we have. I'm not comparing the two of them.

"I know what you mean."

A weight lifts off my shoulders. Saying it out loud, even to one person, feels so much lighter. I can't believe how heavy it felt to treat that information as a terrible secret. I can't count how many nights I've lain awake wondering if I'd told Quincy what she wanted to hear, if I'd allowed myself to acknowledge it, would she still be alive?

What-ifs have never healed a damn thing, though, as Damon would say. "It was a different love than what we have," I say, realizing what Ella might think and feel in this moment might be the complete opposite of what I'm experiencing.

A smile curves her lips. "I know, Z," she murmurs. Ella maneuvers herself and drops into my lap, but I can feel in the tension of her muscles that she's insecure.

My jailbird belongs to me. Now and always. She shouldn't feel insecure for even a second.

"Come closer." I wrap my arms around her.

"I'm already sitting in your lap," she says with a playful laugh.

Tension thickens between us. A new tension. It makes my heart pound loud in my ears. I brush a lock of her hair back from her face and tuck it behind her ear. Ella's expression turns serious.

"What is it, jailbird?"

I can see the fear in her eyes. She thinks there might be more. Another layer of secrets when it comes to me and Quincy. But she's not able to verbalize the question. I understand. I couldn't talk about this for so long. The longer I went without saying it, the less I believed I could.

"I love you, Ella. I need you to understand."

The fear slowly retreats from her eyes, and she turns pink in the cheeks. The last thing to arrive is a small, trusting smile.

"Now," I say, "be a good girl for me."

"Z," she says, quickly. "I love you too, but—"

"There are no buts." I'm firm, but cut her off before she can complete that thought.

Ella cannot doubt me after everything she's been through. I won't let her do it. Her happiness is mine. Her sadness as well. That means her uncertainty is also mine.

I stand up and gently guide her to remain on the couch. "Lie back."

Ella perches on the edge and leans back, stretching

her body out before me, her eyes glinting. I'm slow and deliberate, testing and teasing her as I go. The fire crackles behind my back and it reflects in her heated gaze. With a single kiss, I tell her that I love her again.

Ever so slowly, I push her slip to her hips, letting the silk ride up her thighs. She shivers from the contact and her nipples pebble under the thin fabric. I groan as I pull her panties to the side and put my mouth between her legs, taking a languid lick. Her fingers splay through my hair and her back bows slightly.

It's more of the connection I've been craving since I decided to tell her. I needed this. The taste of her is everything I needed.

I'm overwhelmed with a sense of peace. It was the right decision to tell her. I've made it my business to know as much as I can about Ella. While I may be her Dom in the bedroom, that doesn't mean we're unequal. Some people new to the lifestyle can make the mistake of thinking that subs are lesser than Doms. That they have less influence in the relationship.

It's not true. She's just as important as I am. Even more so. Sharing myself with her is as crucial as Ella sharing all her deepest secrets with me.

Licking and sucking her clit, while she gasps and cries out, sends even more desire through me.

Ella's slick and hot, and her thighs clench around

my shoulders.

It won't be long now.

Her fingers wind through my hair.

This is the best life has to offer. There's nothing I'd rather do than make Ella come.

I lift my head from her pussy and speak to her as I reach up and pull down one thin strap of her silk slip. Her full breast fits perfectly in my hand and I massage her, commanding her, "Come for me, jailbird."

The second my tongue touches her again and I pinch her nipple ever so slightly, Ella comes in a burst of pleasure. She hangs on to the couch cushions for dear life. Her nails scrape against the fabric as she cries out my name.

She's still coming when someone steps into the room. The footsteps only resonate with the sound of, "Shit, fuck. I'm sorry." The words all tumble out rapid fire. It's my fucking brother.

Ella gasps, curling up into a ball to cover herself and I turn, wiping her arousal off on my shirt to face Cade.

"I'm sorry," he says with his hands raised, "I didn't see anything."

His widened eyes tell me he's lying. "Out. Get out." A possessiveness I haven't felt before comes over me. Damon's seen me fuck Ella. But I knew he was there. There was permission. There was pleasure given to my

Ella. This was not that.

"Of course," he says and turns abruptly. Cade leaves the living room, his footsteps quickly growing quieter.

I gather Ella into my arms, put her on her feet, and rearrange her clothes. "Go upstairs, jailbird. Wait for me in bed. I need more from you than that."

"Z," she says, her eyes darting to the threshold of the room.

"It's all right." I take her jaw in my hand, pull her face to mine, and kiss her hard. She moans as she tastes herself on my lips. The connection burns between us, strong and raw.

After she's upstairs and her bedroom door has closed, I go to find Cade in the kitchen. He's leaning against the counter, his hands in his pockets.

"You need to contain yourself, Zander."

"No," I snap. "I'll be fucking her on every inch of furniture. On every inch of the floor. I'm going to make that woman feel alive and loved and wanted."

His eyes narrow, but there's a thoughtful expression behind them.

My anger is as hot as my love for her right now. It's even stronger now that I've had a chance to let go of the bitter grief I've been holding onto for so, so long. "I mean it, Cade. I'm going to fuck her whenever I want. Wherever I want. Until all her sadness is gone and the past takes its claws all the way out of her. And as for *you,* you need to send a damn text before you come over."

Cade stares for a moment, shaking his head as if I've lost my mind. His expression shifts and he nods, slapping a stack of papers down on the kitchen counter. "Fine. I can send a text. I'll send a text next time I'm going to stop by, but you need to see this."

I go to his side, forcing myself to calm down, and look at the papers. "What are these?" I flick through them. They appear to be medical reports ... news articles. It's a mix of papers with several lines highlighted. Including "strangulation" but then "death by suicide."

"What the hell are these?"

"This is what you asked Silas to research." He folds his arms over his chest. "Ella's mother didn't die by suicide."

We both look down at the documents together. The awkwardness of the past moment is forgotten. I flip through the papers, then again.

"There are a lot of things that don't add up," Cade says to my right as I read.

I'm reminded of the conversation I had with Kam a few nights ago. "Kamden told me he thinks her father did it."

"Why would he tell you that?" Cade sounds skeptical. He's rarely ever thrown off his game, but this is bothering him. "And how, exactly, would he know that?"

The front door opens, then bangs shut. "Hello?"

Kamden calls.

The fact is, I don't know what's going on. But Kam's footsteps come closer by the second. I use the time to lean in close and murmur something to my brother. "I think it's time the cameras came down."

Kam steps into the kitchen then. Crossing swiftly to the island, he drops a box of pastries onto the counter. Cade locks eyes with me and gives me a single, silent nod.

Chapter 6

Ella

It's a rotation.

Damon, Zander, Kam, Zander, Silas, Zander. Occasionally Dane. Zander is a constant but gives them space. And they take shifts watching, questioning, and observing every little thing I do more often than not.

Men revolve around me and I'm held accountable to each of them. Any slight stress from any of the men monitoring me is immediately alleviated by Z.

In a past life, I'd have resented all of them. I'd have pitched a fit and fought tooth and nail for privacy and freedom. Even Kamden for interfering, for being overbearing, for not leaving me the hell alone, would be on the receiving end of my wrath. But this go-around? I look forward to the sessions, the questions, the appointments. Maybe it's because they're all I have left. Or maybe it's because Z is there at the end of all of them, rewarding me and reminding me that none of this matters.

As I stir sugar into my tea, Kam shuffles the papers on the counter next to me. He has stacks laid out along the granite. This is cup two for me and the steam billows outward as I blow across the top. The mug itself is a present Kam gave me only two hours ago when he arrived. A pearl blue iridescent mug that's limited edition from Tiffany.

"I can't help but think you're trying to butter me up."

"I wish," Kam answers absently as he shuffles through the papers. He doesn't look back at me, very much consumed with the next line of business.

Shifting on the stool, I'm careful to gather the fabric of my skirt so it doesn't bunch. It's a classic navy blue high-waisted number and I paired it with a simple short-sleeved white blouse that's loosely tucked in. I decided to attempt to look as if I'm prepared for business, even if in reality I won't be leaving the house and I could have stayed in my pajamas from yesterday.

I rock gently to and fro on the stool, watching Kam squint at the papers until he pulls out his glasses from his shirt pocket.

With the slacks and thin wire-rimmed glasses he

reminds me of his father for a moment. He was a hedge fund manager and as Kam gets older, he looks more and more like him. Not that I would tell him that. He hated his father and for good reason. For similar reasons that I hated mine.

"We have three offers but we shouldn't take any on the beach house. The one in LA you may want to consider, but I wouldn't say yes to anything yet."

His statement makes me pause the easy motion of back and forth. "I'm sorry, did you say 'offers?' How do we have bids if we haven't put them on the market?"

His glasses clink as he closes them and then he passes me three papers. I don't bother looking at them, he'll explain it well enough. "We haven't put them up on the market, but some realtors have contacted me. There's clear interest but I thought maybe we should wait until you can see them one last time. Make sure that you are set on selling them?"

My heart does a little tumble and my fingertips go numb. I take a sip of tea, allowing it to warm my hands instead of replying.

If I were to go to those homes, especially the beach house, all I would see are memories of James. Even now, without stepping foot on the premises, I see him.

"I'd rather just sell them," I tell Kam with finality and set the mug down. Memories flood in and I can't shove them away.

"You don't want to say goodbye? Have a look around? We'd be selling fully furnished and I don't want you to regret that. Or regret anything."

I remember the moment James and I bought our first house together in LA. I remember the snapshot we took, how he kissed my cheek and whispered, *I love you, my wild girl.*

Tears prick as I imagine never setting foot in the same bedroom where he made love to me, the same kitchen where he told me he loved me for the first time.

"Is it bad if I don't?" I ask Kam and steady myself. I'm not going to cry. Not over houses and furniture. This is the home we spent the least amount of time in. We bought it because of the bedrooms. We wanted a family. And that family will never happen now. It was only hopeful wishes that lived here and they have since been replaced by reality.

"Not at all," Kam is quick to answer and then offers, "Do you want pictures of any of them?"

"Pictures?"

"I had a photographer take photos of everything in the houses... if you want to see them to have a look over? Especially the items left behind. Is there anything at all you can think of that you don't want sold with the properties?"

My answer is immediate. "There's a picture by the bed in the beach house."

The moment the statement leaves me, Kamden gives his complete attention to a manila envelope and takes out a bundle of photos held together with a paper clip.

I glance, but just as quickly return my attention back to the mug in front of me. The nervous energy doesn't leave me alone. Neither do all the memories.

"This one?" he asks, handing me a printout of what could be a home decor magazine cover. I forgot how much we spent decorating that house to make it perfect. I forgot how luxurious it looked. The painting by James's bedside was a gift I gave him the weekend before we got married.

He wanted to elope on an island off of the coast. I didn't and he caved easily, telling me we could do whatever I wanted. The weekend before the wedding, which was set in an expensive hotel in Maui, we took a jet out to that island where in a simple white sundress, I told him my vows and Kam married us. Trish snapped the photo and my artist friend made it into a painting.

We both got the wedding of our dreams and none of our guests beyond our inner circle knew there were two.

That painting is a secret and a memory and it's exactly who we were as a couple.

"I just want that painting, please," I whisper to Kam

and touch ever so gently at the corner of my eye, willing the tear not to fall. I remind myself that I am okay and there's no reason to cry. It's fine. Everything is fine.

"Of course," Kam answers and he can't hide the sympathy in his voice.

That's what does it; the damn tear falls. "I think I want to see Zander," I manage to get out with my throat tight. Rule three. Rule three.

"Okay ... is there something I can do?"

"Just get him, please," I plead with him as my shoulders tremble. I don't want to cry anymore. But if I must, something inside of me simply needs Z to hold me while I do. When he holds me, it ends when the tears stop. If he's not there ... I spiral.

"I would do anything for you."

"I know. I would do anything for you too."

"Okay, let's go see Zander. The rest of this can wait."

With deep breaths, I push the stool out, the legs scraping against the floor. "Let me help you," Kam offers with a hand on my elbow at the same time that the front door opens and Trish can be heard calling out, "Honey, I'm home!"

"Shit," Kam mutters under his breath and then reaches for a cloth napkin, handing it to me to dry my unwanted tears.

"Do you want me to get rid of her?" he questions

beneath his breath as her keys jingle closer and closer to us. "Anyone home?" she calls out.

With a weak smile, I shake my head no. "No. It's okay. I'm okay," I'm quick to push out the words, all the while sniffling and trying to shut down the sudden grief.

I'll have to tell Zander, though. He needs to know. My thoughts are cut off by a concerned voice.

"Oh my God ... are you crying?" Trish stands in the opening to the kitchen, keys in one hand, a box from pastries from my favorite local bakery in the other with her purse dangling from the crook of her elbow. In white skinny jeans and a simple navy top with a white minimalist logo, we actually match. It's the same colors, just inverted, and I'm uptown while she's downtown chic.

"I like your shoes," I answer her and then shrug at her question. She takes a peek down at her pointed toe navy heels before looking back up to me. "Oh, my love," she says and pouts. "No deflecting. Tell me, what's the matter?"

"I'll get tissues until you two are ready for retail therapy," Kam says and leaves the two of us to hug awkwardly with Trish's hands still full.

Wiping my eyes and sniffling I tell her it's the same old, same old.

I let out a weak laugh as she unloads on the counter and then she hugs me for real. One of the strong kind that can hold you up when you want to collapse.

"I swear I'm all right," I tell her, blotting under my eyes with the tissue Kam gives me and then accepting another for my nose.

"You had a moment," Kam says and looks to his sister. "It was just a moment."

It's odd how the smallest things set me off. "I wish I could just stop it."

"It'll come and go, babe. There's no stopping grief."

I nod as he talks, feeling calmer by the second. Trish stares at me and I can feel her gaze, but I focus on deep breaths.

"It was a fast moment," Kam adds and this time I say, "That damn ball in the box."

All Trish says is, "Fuck that ball," in the driest, most sarcastic tone I've heard in a long time and I can't help but to laugh. "I don't know anything about it but it can fuck right off."

Her comment makes me laugh and Kam pats my hand.

"Does my makeup still look okay," I ask her and she tilts her head slightly, taking the tissue from me. "Let me just ..." she says and I chuckle again.

"I'm such a mess."

"You okay?" she asks with an empathetic pout, rubbing my back once the laugh is over.

Nodding, I crumple up the tissues and tell her, "Yeah.

I was just …"

"Just grieving," Kam finishes for me and I nod again in agreement.

"I have a distraction if you'd like," Trish offers, pulling out the stool Kam previously sat in. She misses the comical glare he gives her and I nearly laugh again but it's cut off when she says, "Did you see what the tabloids said?" Without waiting for me to answer, she turns to her brother to ask, "Did you tell her?"

As he shakes his head I ask deadpan, "Am I the reckless rich bitch whore again?"

"Not quite," she says and passes me her phone.

"We didn't make a statement, right?" I clarify with Kam and he nods, confirming, but then says, "They decided no statement was a sign that there's love in the air."

The first reads: *Crazy Meets Crazy, Heated Forbidden Romance!* and then I swipe right to read the second one: *He May Be Her Bodyguard but Her Body Isn't Guarded From Him …*

Just beneath the second headline is a picture of me, soaking wet from head to toe, my bra visible beneath my dress as I grip onto Z and he looks down at me as if we're about to kiss.

Did we? It was at the party; tensions were high, emotions even higher. I barely remember that moment. From the picture, though, it looks as if it's a still from a romance movie. As if we're about to kiss against the wall.

His expression is everything. It reads pure devotion.

"For real I thought he might have fucked you against that wall right then and there in front of everyone," Trish jokes.

"If you could refrain from that, the PR team would appreciate it," Kam comments dryly.

Trish laughs first and then I follow. For a moment, for one small moment everything feels like it used to. Then I hand her phone back and I remember it's nothing like it used to be.

"You looked like you might be in love," Trish says but her tone is slightly defeated as she watches me war with myself. I know my expression doesn't hide a thing.

"So ... are you two in love?" she presses lightheartedly and Kam mutters beneath his breath for her to leave me alone as he stacks all the papers on the counter back into one pile.

I don't answer her but I know the truth. I love the way he makes me feel and I want him to feel this way too.

"You good?" Kam asks.

I hesitate to answer, glancing at Trish and then back to Kam. "... I'm better."

With a rap of his knuckles, Zander stands on the other side of the glass. Tall, dark and handsome, in gray slacks and a thin black tie, he peeks in the window waiting rather than pulling back the sliding glass door beside him. I huff a small laugh as he looks through the window and signals by pointing to his chest. It means: *Do you need me?*

I blow him a kiss back. It's our code for: *I'm all right.* There's a sputtering in my chest as I'm caught in his gaze. It strikes me that he could have walked another few steps, but where he's standing would be the first place he'd be able to see me.

"Your knight in shining armor for real," Trish comments.

"I might have messaged him," Kam admits. He adds, "I can keep her occupied if you want to see him?"

"I'm 'her' now?" Trish jokes at the same time that I respond.

"I'm good." Z smiles at me through the window, gives a short wave and then goes back to the deck where he's been talking with Damon. They're making plans to present paperwork to the judge. Something that has to happen for the conservatorship to dissolve. It's all so heavy and I wish it was just over with legally.

"That's cute that he checks on you," Trish states and then opens up the box from the French bakery I love downtown. She offers me a tiny cupcake but I wave it away. As does Kam. With a shrug, she leans back and bites into her morsel.

The emotions swing so wildly, I don't know what to think anymore.

"It's going to be okay, isn't it?" I question Kam because he knows it all. He takes a moment, observing me and not answering right away. "I don't know why I feel like this," I admit out loud.

"Do we need to—" he starts and I can see the panic and worry in his gaze.

I cut him off, not wanting to cause him more stress than I already have. "This is me telling my friend ... I don't know why I can't trust it. I think the moment I'm happy it's going to be ripped from me."

"Nothing is going to be taken from you," Kam says, attempting to comfort me but it doesn't work.

"If I let myself fall for him and then ... something happens and he's gone ..." I can barely get the words out. It's the first time I've said it out loud. "I can't go through that again."

Kam's answer strikes me hard, although his voice is nearly a whisper. "What happened to James was an accident, Ella."

"I know. I know."

"It was a fucking tragedy," Trish adds.

"You deserve to be happy," Kam tells me with a gentle firmness. "He makes you happy, doesn't he?"

"He does," I answer.

"And he loves you," Trish points out.

"He does," I say with a simper, letting the warmth flood me. Not fighting it and knowing it's true. He does.

"You love him?" Trish asks.

"I do."

Kam steps in, placing a hand on each of my shoulders and says, "Then be happy. For fuck's sake, Ella, be happy. That's all anyone wants and you never know when it's all going to change. One moment and everything falls. We've seen it so many times. We recover, we always do. I will always make sure you get back up. But you're up, babe. You can be happy now. I promise you."

Chapter 7

Zander

Ella's been doing exceptionally well. Much better than I ever could have imagined that first day I saw her in the courtroom. She still has moments, but she acknowledges them, embraces them and then gives them to me.

She's fucking perfect.

All I've done today is praise her in the playroom. Anticipation coats the air. All of the equipment is arranged as it usually is. Ella stands naked in the middle of the room, preparing herself. It's like other scenes we've done.

The difference this time is that there's a camera. The steady red light from atop the dresser indicates everything we do is being recorded.

I've ordered Ella not to look at it. I want her attention solely on me.

Still, it's like another person is in the room with us, watching.

Her chest rises heavily, lust evident in her expression. She loves this. And I can give it to her so easily.

It's not my kink, to be watched, but I can't say that it doesn't thrill me. She loved it when I fucked her on that chair with another actual person in the room. The camera is a stand-in for that feeling, yes, but it's also serving another important purpose.

I want this documented so that she can see.

Ella deserves the right to see everything we do together the way I see it, or the way an onlooker would see it. By using the camera, I'm making that possible for her.

The new addition makes the session feel more charged, like she has a willing audience ready to play into her exhibitionist tendencies. Even if nobody's watching on a screen in another room.

It's also an avenue for something she's unaware of. It's for me to delve deeper into territories that may be uncomfortable. Things I may need Damon's help addressing.

I have her body. I want all of her, though. Every bit and that requires asking questions that may trigger her.

Swallowing thickly, a paddle in my hand, I stare into

Ella's dark eyes and steady myself. She breathes heavily, her face flushed from already having pleasured herself. A vibrator is on the floor at her bare feet.

Slowly, I tie her hands and attach them to the hook above her head as I speak. "I'm going to ask you questions. You remember your safe word, don't you?"

"Yes," she answers easily, her warm breath tickling my neck as she does. I kiss her hard, my hand falling to her waist.

"What is it?"

"Pink," she says. Taking one step back, I tell her she's a good girl and then I ask in a clear and controlled manner, "What would James tell me about you if I asked him for advice about being your Dom?"

She swallows hard, and I wait patiently. Talking about James is difficult for Ella, but she's been getting better at it. What I've learned about painful topics is that staying silent about them doesn't work. Not in the long run. I learned that from talking to Ella about Quincy. Repetition and exposure are the only things that make it easier. Not less painful, really, but easier.

James shouldn't be a dark secret. Not between us. No dark secrets belong in a relationship like ours. Doing this will only bring us closer.

A faint smile comes to her face, and inwardly I sigh with relief.

"He would say ..." Ella begins slowly but thoughtfully. She rests her weight on the cuffs at her wrists, and I can tell she's weighing each word as well. "He would say that I respond well to praise."

That's right. She does. I give her a nod of encouragement.

"And he would say that maybe a little degradation works too. He would say that I need a firm hand." She smirks slightly, still looking at me.

"You do need a firm hand," I agree. "You test my patience sometimes, don't you?"

"I did in the beginning but I could do a better job of that now," she teases me and my cock hardens.

"Oh, don't push me right now, my little bird, not when I have a new ... kink to test with you."

Her dark eyes brighten. I don't put a collar around her neck. Not yet. I use my hand instead. "Do you trust me?" Her pulse is hot against my skin.

Ella seems to relax into my grip. "Yes, sir," she answers.

"Do you remember your safe word?" I ask again.

"Yes, sir." Her voice is soft, almost a whisper, but she doesn't falter with her words.

I add pressure to my grip, careful to avoid her windpipe. Some think choking is about the throat. It's not. That's dangerous and more than a little damaging. I only put a small amount of pressure on her carotid artery. It'll make Ella light-headed, and heighten the pleasure. "Eyes open and on me," I command her, barely squeezing, only testing. Her dark gaze stays on mine as I add a bit more pressure.

Her nipples pebble and a blush flushes her skin.

"How much do you trust me?" I ask.

"With my life," she says.

"You know that's in my hands right now, don't you?" I ask.

"Yes, sir," she says.

"Do you like that feeling, jailbird?"

"Yes, sir," she whispers, but I already know she does. Her body writhes as she hangs helplessly for me. Bending down, I flick the vibrator on and I press it between her legs. Her back bows slightly.

"Be still, Ella," I command, leaving no room in my tone for argument, "and keep your eyes open." She does as instructed and the moment I find that sweet spot, I know it. Her bottom lip drops and strangled moans leave her. I murmur, "There it is."

With my left hand controlling the wand and the right back at her throat, I give her pleasure like she's never felt before.

I put a little more pressure on until her pupils expand and she struggles to stay still. "Come for me, Ella," I whisper, holding her gaze.

"Oh," she says in a breathy voice and her toes curl, making her entire body sway as she loses her balance.

"Light-headed?" I ask, checking in.

"Yes," she says. "I almost feel ..."

"High?"

"Yes," she answers. "It feels good," she adds and she's far too calm, so I turn up the vibrations with the press of my thumb. As her lips form a perfect O, I question, "Being choked?"

"No," she struggles to answer and then pushes out the next statement in a rush. "You having so much control."

I arch an eyebrow at her. "Sir," she finishes, the one word a pitch higher as her head falls back. I keep the pressure steady, feeling her pulse pound beneath my fingers and let her come. And she does, so beautifully. My cock twitches with need at the sight of her, lost in pleasure.

She heaves in a breath after I take my hand away from her neck. "Now stay still, my good girl."

I step back and watch her struggle to compose herself. She's already come twice and I imagine a third is going to wear her out. I'm aiming for four, though.

Pulling a small silver clicker out of my pocket, I tell her, "One click equals one spank." Her eyes fly open wide and she readjusts herself, paying attention. I raise the clicker in the air and press my thumb down. "There's one. I told you to be still."

This is a simple game, but it'll be difficult for her and we both know it. I'm setting her up to fail, but she will love being disciplined and it keeps her from being tempted to talk back, to disobey in any way. She'll enjoy the sweet pain of punishment as often as she needs.

Because I will set her up to fail. She needs it.

Ella attempts to stay still, but she bites at her lip watching me. "There's two. Keep your eyes on me," I tell her, releasing the bonds from above her head. "Stay still with your arms at your side." I lower each, rubbing her wrists as I do.

Her hands are resting loosely by her sides, but as I watch her, as I take in her beautiful naked body, one of her fingers flexes. "There's three," I say and she swallows audibly.

I make her stand there for three minutes as I pace around her. Kissing where I'd like and checking her wrists and throat. It must feel like an eternity. For the person trying to stay still, of course it does. Staying still isn't a hardship until someone else orders you to do it. It's easy until you have to.

By the time the three minutes is up, Ella is trembling. I don't count that against her. That's just her muscles. In all, she's earned herself thirteen spanks.

The bed groans as I sit on the edge of it, my cock

eager to be buried inside of her. I could have her ride the horse or the bench, but I crave her like this for tonight.

"Now come here," I say. She nods and does as she's told, her bare feet padding against the floor. When she reaches me, I pull her over my lap. "I don't want you to count," I tell her. "I'll keep track. You take your punishment like a good girl."

Ella gasps loudly at the first swat, her hands fisting. I don't hold back but I soothe the spot the moment it's done.

That small touch is rewarded with a moan, reminding me how eager I am to be inside of her. With another swat and then another, my breath quickens with eagerness.

She squirms slightly, and muffles her cries as I spank her ass again and again.

At the end of thirteen, her ass is red and there are tears on her cheeks. I press my fingers against her and then slip them inside of her, stroking her front wall. Her moan is fucking heaven. It's then I see a tear fall.

"You did so well," I praise her and remove my fingers only to rub a hand over her glowing skin. "Are you hurt?"

She shakes her head and then tells me no.

"These are good tears then?" I question, leaning down to kiss her cheek. "Yes," she answers and I soothe her ass again before telling her, "Now it's time to stand up."

I help her to her feet, and Ella wobbles a bit as she finds her balance. She pulls herself upright and looks me in the eyes without wiping the tears from her face. So I do it for her.

"Ask me something," I say. "Ask me while the camera's watching."

"I'm not sure what to ask," she says. "I just want to touch you."

"Keep your hands at your sides," I say and to ease the immediate disappointment, I add, "You can touch me later."

"What's your favorite thing about me?" Ella asks after a moment.

"How red your ass is right now," I joke but then I tell her, "How I feel like this was meant to be. Like there isn't another person in this world that could want me and need me exactly how I want and need you."

Ella thinks for a minute. "Do you ever wish you could go back?"

No.

There's a chill that spreads over every inch of my skin. I know the answer right away, but I don't want her to think I'm telling her what she wants to hear.

If I had the chance, would I go back? Would I try to change things?

The answer is still the same.

"No, jailbird. I wouldn't. How could you even think that?"

Her head shakes softly and she swallows audibly. Her bottom lip quivers and before she can say anything, I pick her up and toss her on the bed onto her knees. Lowering my lips to the shell of her ear, I tell her, "I'm going to fuck that thought out of your pretty little head and you're never allowed to think it again."

As I slam inside of her to the hilt and she struggles to stay upright, I remind her, "You are mine and I'm exactly who you're meant to belong to."

I almost add "right now" but the words stop short. She is mine and she will stay mine. That is all that matters.

Chapter 8

Ella

Every time he looks at me like that, nothing else exists.

It seems to get more intense as the nights go on. Four nights in a row now, we've spent our evenings in the playroom. Tonight we're in my bedroom, but with that look, we might as well be in the playroom.

"Kiss me," he says. The command is roughly ordered and I obey immediately.

Every small touch seems longer as time seems to slow. Heat and want dance along every inch of my skin. His fingers barely graze my curves as he breaks the kiss. I shiver from the touch and then bite down on my lower lip, peeking up at him and waiting.

He doesn't make me wait long.

"Strip." The singular word is deadly on his lips.

His hungry gaze watches me and I take my time, making my motions as seductive as possible. Slowly tugging the fabric off and watching as his gaze roams down my body in longing. My bra unclasps easily enough and he licks his lower lip watching my nipples harden as wisps of cool air caress my skin.

As the last piece falls into the puddle of fabric, he groans, his right hand flexing and his gaze finally coming back to mine.

He murmurs in contemplation, "What toy do I want to use on you tonight?"

With one step forward, I dare to take a bit of control.

"Do we need toys?" I question, reaching down and gripping his already hardened length through his slacks. "I just need you inside of me."

"My greedy girl," he says and I swear it's the sexiest thing I've ever heard. With lust reflecting in his eyes, all I want is more. More of his praise. More of his touch. Anything that involves more of *him*.

"Your good girl too, aren't I?" I whisper, maintaining eye contact all the while, and drop to my knees in front of him. The carpet is rough against my knees and I don't care. My breathing is heavy and I'm careful not to fumble as I unbutton his slacks, then tug the zipper down.

With a heavy groaned exhale coated in desire, Zander

spears his fingers through my hair while his other hand helps me pull down his pants and boxers all at once.

The instant I'm able, the head of his cock is in my mouth. I moan around him, sucking the bit of salty precum from the tip and then massaging my tongue against the underside of his cock.

His hand wraps around the back of my neck as I take more of him into my mouth, all the way to the back of my throat.

"Fuck, Ella," he hisses and warmth flows through me. I hollow my cheeks, giving him pleasure. My nipples pebble from the chill of the room and I love it. I love this. I love him.

His cock presses against the back of my throat and I nearly gag on him, but I don't stop. I'm far too eager to please him.

He permits this for only a moment before surprising me by yanking me up and tossing me onto the bed. It seems so effortless for him as I bounce slightly and then sink into the luxurious sheets.

My chest rises and falls as he climbs onto the bed after me. His broad shoulders are carved from pure muscle and the sight of him staring at me as if he wants nothing more in his entire life leaves me breathless.

He breaks my gaze only to grab the pillow behind me.

"Spread your legs for me," he orders while placing

the pillow under the small of my back. I do as I'm told, allowing him to position me however he wants while every nerve ending lights with fire in anticipation of what he's going to do to me.

Of course I obey him, spreading my legs for his hips to fit exactly where I need them, but he grips my upper thighs and pushes them back further, pinning me in an angled position so he can see my pussy easily. As my heated skin tingles in anticipation, he lowers himself, groaning as he takes a languid lick of my slit. His hungry eyes reach mine after sucking on my clit. They're dark and foreboding.

"When you come, you're going to thank me. Do you understand?"

Nodding, I eagerly agree. "I'll thank you."

"Good girl," he tells me before lowering his face back to my clit. He's unforgiving as he massages his tongue against my hardened nub. The vibrations of his groans of desire spread goosebumps up my skin as the pleasure hits me like waves crashing against the shore. More and more intense until I'm desperate for my release.

"Zander, please," I beg him and he lets go of my thigh to press two fingers inside of me, curving them and ruthlessly stroking my G-spot. I come recklessly under him. My climax is violent and arrives faster than I could have expected.

Even still, I thank him like he told me to do.

I spread my legs for him but he pushes my thighs up higher and pins them back. Fuck. He angles me and thrusts in deep. Deeper than he's been before and heat engulfs me. "Z," I say. There's a plea in my voice I can't help.

He leans forward, his hard body against mine and groans, "So fucking tight but I'll loosen you up." As he rocks, the pleasure builds and his pubes rubbing against my clit only heighten everything. Lighting every nerve ending aflame.

My heart pounds in my chest as the intensity climbs.

Every thrust pushes me higher and higher.

Every glance up his hazel eyes are on mine.

Every kiss silences desperate cries of pleasures. And all the while my heart races, my blood heats and the words "I love you" threaten to spill from my lips.

I resist which makes it all the more surprising and emotional when he whispers at the shell of my ear as I drift off to sleep in his arms, sated and spent, "Thank you for loving me."

There's a *tick*, *tick*, in my chest as I pretend to be sleeping. I'm falling, I know I'm falling and I'm fucking terrified of what that means and mostly, of ever losing him.

Chapter 9

Zander

The comparison of Ella's home to mine is night and day. That's all I can think as I fill her fridge with groceries that are meant for both of us. Sports drinks all in a row line the bottom shelf of the fridge and they're for me, not her. I've practically moved in and there's a piece of me that's unsettled in doing so. There are so many loose ends that need to be tied up. The sound of someone coming through the back door steals my attention.

It's Kamden. His expression appears wary, almost angry.

"Hey," he says, shutting the door behind him. "Are you busy?"

"Just putting these away." I hold up a gallon of milk

and then turn my back to him, opening up the door and asking, "Something you wanted to talk about?"

My hackles bristle whenever he's around. I'm not sure if it's possessiveness or if it's because he knows more about Ella than I do. Or because there are secrets between us, but I know he loves Ella. I know he'd do anything for her. The possessiveness rises again. I don't know if that makes him an ally or an enemy.

"Yes. There's something we need to discuss." He hovers around the table in the breakfast nook, seeming unable to make up his mind about whether he should sit or stand for this conversation.

I don't like it. Kam is a bit of a wild card in this situation, and I'm still not sure what to think about him.

"Whatever you need to talk to me about, just say it. Ella's upstairs resting." I finish putting the groceries in the fridge and face him.

Kamden's eyes darken. "It's about the cameras."

"I don't work for The Firm anymore," I say and then gesture. "This place doesn't need to be full of cameras."

"Yeah. So I saw." Kam pulls up his phone and taps the screen. There's a video of me removing the cameras. Well, fuck.

"What is it? Did you want to see us fucking?"

He rolls his eyes and drops his arm. "I want to see her safe. That's what I want."

He's not as angry as I expected he'd be. Not even with me being kind of a prick. There's an uneasiness about him, but that's not necessarily a sign he's working against us.

"Look, I just ... I need to know she's safe. All right. You could have at least given me a heads-up before you made that change."

"Sorry." I can understand what that's like. It makes me soften toward him. Maybe he does want what's best for her. "I'll keep her safe," I add, and I sure as hell mean that. It's a promise.

Kam nods like he believes me. He finally sits down at the kitchen table, but he's restless like he hasn't said all he wanted to say yet. His foot taps. He opens his mouth, then he shuts it again. I keep my eyes on him and wait. People who want to talk will always open up if you stay quiet and give them the space they need.

Kam lets out a rough breath and narrows his eyes at me, a thoughtful expression on his face. "At first I thought you were into her because of the money."

My eyebrows quirk up but I stay silent.

"I looked into your finances," he explains. "Found something interesting."

"You found out about the insurance," I guess.

"Yes. I found out," Kam continues, "that you're wealthy in your own right ... from Quincy's death, but you don't seem to have touched any of it."

I swallow hard at the mention of her name. I've never touched it for a reason. Even now, I'm technically unemployed but I haven't had to dip into it yet, and I don't know that I want to. I'm immediately uncomfortable at having Kam say it out loud, but I sit with the emotion rather than letting it turn to anger. I do have enough money to last a lifetime if it's managed correctly. The fact that Kam knows about it doesn't change anything.

"No," I tell him. "I haven't touched a dime."

He studies me for a few seconds. "I don't know what to think of you, Zander."

"And I don't know what to think of you."

"Yes, you do." Now he's exasperated. The anger reappears in his eyes. Or is it just frustration? It could go either way. "I'm someone who will do anything to protect her. Anything."

"And?"

"And I'm willing to let in others who will do the same." He looks at me intently, willing me to respond.

"Or," I counter, "you're someone who won't mind pushing people out if you think they've gotten too close."

Kam smirks at me. "You're more like James than I realized. More bitter, I think. James didn't hold on to things like you do."

He's genuinely angry by the time he's done speaking.

His face is turning a little red. He opens his jacket and pulls out a bottle of alcohol.

"Ella's not allowed to have that here," I tell him, my voice hard.

"She's not an alcoholic," he says and then adds, "This is for me, though." After a swig, he eyes me. "I'm not an alcoholic. Do I cope with it? Do I misuse it at times? ... I'm working on it. Spare me your judgment."

"Drink all you'd like. I just don't want Ella to have it."

"Yeah." Surprisingly he agrees and Kam motions with the bottle. "I know there's an association between misuse and..." He hesitates and the color drains from his face.

"Suicidal thoughts." I complete the sentence for him.

Kam nods and then says, "I don't know if you know, but when she gets like this, it fucks me up a bit."

I watch him. Carefully this time.

Kam unscrews the top and tips back the bottle. After taking a pull he offers it to me, but I decline with a gesture.

"When she gets like this?" I question. "You say that like it happens often."

Kam lets out a sarcastic huff. "I thought we were bonding here."

I give him a humorless laugh in return. There's a moment of silence. Kam has another swig as I look out the back window. He didn't drive here, because there's no car outside. He walked.

That must mean he was fucked up before he came. He wasn't planning to drive. That's one point in his favor. If he'd driven here, drunk behind the wheel—

"Nobody drunk should ever be behind the wheel, especially not if they're fucked up," Kam says, as if he can read my mind. He stares into the distance and I watch the memories go through his eyes as he takes another sip from his bottle.

Nerves have me on edge. "You all right?" I ask him.

"I've just been thinking," he answers.

"About what?"

"Just what she's been through." Kam was the one to witness it all firsthand.

"It wasn't just after James died," he says after a while, abruptly, like he snapped back to bonding with me. Or like this is too heavy for him to keep inside anymore. "She had a difficult life."

I think about all the information Cade gave me. All those files.

Slowly, I pull out a chair at the table and take a seat with him.

I take a moment to study him. He came here with alcohol in his jacket pocket, and he's been talking openly about her rough childhood. I don't know what has him so upset, but maybe if I just listen, he'll feel like elaborating.

"Her childhood wasn't her fault," he says and then finishes the bottle.

But what if Kam thinks he has some responsibility for that? If he blames himself for things that happened to her, then it would explain how he's behaving right now. If he was involved in how things played out for her, even more so.

I'm not sure how to press him for details. I haven't worked with Kam like that. Taking a deep breath, I settle on acknowledging the obvious.

"From what I've heard, it was pretty rough."

"'Pretty rough' is putting it mildly," he comments. I wonder if he's only telling me this because he knows that I'm looking into it.

"You know what happened to her mom?" he asks.

"Yes," I say, searching his gaze. "Is there something else you want to tell me about that? Maybe something I don't know?"

Kam looks at me for a long, long time. Too long of a moment passes and then he runs a hand down his face. "No," he says finally. "I just wanted to talk. I just wanted to ask you about the cameras."

It already seems like a year ago that he asked me about those cameras. That was his pretense for showing up. It barely lasted five minutes.

"You sure?" I question.

He hesitates for a beat. "Yeah. Will you give me a heads-up first next time you plan to change something major? Just so I know?"

Nodding, I tell him, "I can do that."

"I think I shouldn't have had that last drink," he mutters while rubbing the back of his head.

"You want a ride back home?" I offer and he stares at me for a long moment once again.

Kam stands up from his seat at the table, answering "no" and tucks the empty bottle back into his jacket pocket. He glances toward the staircase. "I'm going to head out. Tell Ella I said hi."

Chapter 10

Ella

The hum of the engine and the brisk wind are more relaxing than I could have imagined. I've been down on this road so many times, but I've never just driven. With the window rolled down, the wind rushes between my fingers and the hint of a smile graces my lips. We round another corner of the long, winding road of the mountain. Nothing but gorgeous foliage and mountainscapes to see.

"You were right. It is a nice drive."

"I like the sound of you telling me I'm right," Z comments, twisting his strong hands on the leather steering wheel.

He glances at me with a wicked look in his eyes and

a cocky grin.

We're both dressed casually. In jeans and T-shirts, like a normal couple on a normal day. Even still, he's devilishly handsome with that perfect smile and rough stubble.

For a moment I'm lost in him and then I glance back, a streak of black catching my eye and I see the car behind us. The Firm is still monitoring every move we make.

I don't feel the sinking dread that I used to knowing that I wasn't allowed to be alone. There's a bit of peace to it now, but sometimes I do just want to be alone with Zander.

It's been two solid weeks of us acting like a normal couple. Maybe acting isn't the right word, but I know we're pretending that the therapy sessions, meetings and constant PR calls are normal. There was an emergency hearing from the judge as well, given that our relationship is now public. That gave Kam and Cade a few gray hairs each.

More articles have come out and Kam suggested a PR move. This drive is potentially one of them. He said paparazzi got a heads-up that we'll be out on a twilight drive along the mountainside. Kam said the magazines catching images of me and Zander doing "normal things" would be good for public peace of mind and ease any worries or concerns that I'm unwell or that our relationship is problematic.

One article suggested Z was taking advantage of me. They sensationalized the forbidden aspect of our relationship, intentionally leaving out that his position in The Firm was withdrawn and that he isn't in charge of my care ... at least not legally. That particular article prompted this drive. I didn't expect to love it so much. The peace and quiet. The normalcy of it all.

"What was your life like before me?"

Z glances at me for a moment, then looks back to the road. The trees whip by as we round the corner, making our way up the side of the mountain. "Hectic, always changing." He clears his throat and readjusts his hands on the wheel. "We had jobs back-to-back. I was constantly on one side of the country and then the other. Nothing was ever settled."

I cock a brow and joke, "So you feel like you're settling?"

His first glance carries concern until he sees my smile. "I feel myself wanting to maybe settle down ... for the first time," he clarifies and glances my way. Gauging my expression.

"Shocked to hear that?" he questions with a smirk. My brow is raised, I know that much but I didn't think I was giving so much away.

"Just ... hearing you talk about settling down is new. That's something we haven't really talked about."

"Do you want to?" he asks.

I want him to tell me how it will happen and then make it my reality. I want it to just be. I want us to just be. That's not what I say, though.

"I'm not sure how that can happen with a tail," I comment and gesture behind us.

He groans, relaxing into his seat. "I could gun it," he jokes and at that very moment, I perk up instantly.

"What?" Z notices and I ease the worry in his tone.

"That spot. Go up and to the right," I direct him, patting his arm and doing what I can to contain my excitement.

I recognize everything about this place. The row of trees, the way they disappear and the sharp drop-off that is just on the other side through the rocky climb.

Nostalgia wraps around me and, in a rarity these days, it makes me smile to remember these times.

"Back in my late teens we'd come up here. Park the car," I tell him and the moment his hand is on the gearshift I unbuckle my seat belt and climb out. The brisk air of the mountains is colder than I expected. We're at a higher elevation than back at the house.

"Where are you going?" Z calls out, his door closing with a thud and then he jogs around the front of his car, chasing after me.

I head toward a small bit of brush by the edge of the cliff and it's almost exactly how I remember. My gait is measured but I can't contain this excitement. As Z stops by my side, I'm vaguely aware that Silas parks behind our car.

"What are you up to?" Z questions with a knitted brow but a barely contained smile that must match mine. As I pull my jacket tighter, Z rests an arm around my shoulders and I lean into him.

"Can't you hear it?" I ask him as the rushing water gets louder and louder. Even the fresh smell is memorable. Everything about this place is just the same as I remember.

"A waterfall?" he says, keeping pace with me as I lead him toward the summit of the cliff.

"They would never catch us here." I slip out of his grip to get closer to the edge, the footpath becoming more rock than brush.

"Who are they?" he questions as the trees become sparse and more of the waterfall can be seen. At the top, looking over, it's breathtaking. I remember the feeling of being here, but my memory could never do justice to the actual sight, which is stunning.

I turn to face him but keep walking and say, "Anyone and everyone. It's our safe place." Almost comically, I nearly trip on the last statement, and catch myself before tumbling forward.

With a firm grasp, Z pulls me closer to him. There's

still a good ten feet of nearly flat rock till the edge, but he acts like I could have fallen over.

"Ella," he says, practically reprimanding me and I laugh in response.

"It's fine. I'm fine." I try to shake him off but he's adamant.

"It's dangerous," Zander tells me in a low tone and I know not to push him much.

"Not with you here," I say and take another step forward, but he holds my elbow just enough to keep me from going toward the edge of the waterfall.

The water is gorgeous. The rushing waves reflect the sunlight and everything about this place is peaceful. The white noise, the fresh atmosphere, and the clean yet woodsy smells in the cool air.

Closing my eyes, I imagine this may be what heaven feels like.

"It's dangerous, Ella," he repeats with emphasis and I have to laugh.

"We used to jump," I tell him, the youthful memory bringing a smile to my lips.

"From here?" he says and the shock in his tone is comical to me. I keep my distance, though, so as not to worry him.

Nodding, I keep the smile in place and tell him, "Yeah, from here."

"Why the fuck would you do that?"

I shrug and give him a rueful grin. "Because we were young and dumb and it was here."

"Who's we?"

"Me. Trish. My girlfriends." I shrug again and he wraps an arm around my waist.

"Don't worry. I'm a good listener and I heard you tell me not to jump," I joke, taking his hand in mine.

He roughly chuckles and squeezes my hand back.

"Besides," I say and peek behind Z to where Silas is watching from a short distance away, "I wouldn't want to give your backup a heart attack."

I'm rewarded with another short, rough chuckle.

"What about Kam?" His tone is more serious now although he tries to play it off.

"What about him?"

"Did he ever jump with you?"

"He knows but he's never jumped." I confide in him without thinking twice. Which is dangerous and yet there isn't an ounce of worry in the confession. Although I know I'm on the edge of unraveling something that's been kept tightly wound and should remain that way. "He's picked me up a time or two before, late at night, soaking wet even."

"You trust Kam," he says almost like it's a question. His gaze stays pinned on me, no longer interested in the fall in the least.

"I don't just trust him, I love him and if you knew—" I stop myself before finishing my statement but Zander picks up where I left off. I swear he knows what I'm thinking before I do sometimes.

"If I knew all your secrets …" he starts.

"If you knew all my family's secrets and those of his too …" I say and trail off, then huff humorlessly and look away but not for long.

With his thumb on my chin and his forefinger beneath it, he tilts my head up so I look him in the eye. His gaze is intense and he pauses a moment, searching my eyes for something before confessing, "I'd still love you."

The intensity is all too much. Like something breaking and crumbling apart in a way where it will never be repaired. Something I don't want to be fixed. Something I don't want to think about ever again.

He leans down, his warm breath meeting mine and he nips my bottom lip before capturing my mouth with his, silencing the sudden gasp from the hint of pain.

He's good at that. My Z … my Dom. He excels at silencing the pain.

"That's my girl," he whispers against my lips and I smile.

A warm feeling in the pit of my stomach flutters like butterfly wings as he kisses me once again. Deeply, with longing, then hungrily. I meet his want with my need and deepen the kiss that much more.

Chapter 11

Zander

It's tense as Cade and I sit facing one another on the opposite ends of the meeting table in The Firm's temporary office. Damon's here too. Along with the rest of the guys.

Anxiousness creeps up the back of my neck, but I do everything I can to shake it off. It didn't hit me in the moment, but looking back on it, I'm sure I lost the respect from the members of The Firm. What happened … I'd do it all over again. There's no way I could ever not be with her. She's mine and she's meant to be mine. But that doesn't mean I'm proud of how it happened. Or that I can't acknowledge I made mistakes that put The Firm and even Ella, at risk.

With a steady inhale, I keep my composure and wait for the mandatory meeting to begin. No doubt it was ordered by Judge Martel.

Scanning the room, it's obvious no one is comfortable. We're all a little restless. I can tell by the way Damon taps his foot and keeps checking the large clock on the wall. He's not usually one to get antsy about meetings, but he's right now, he's impatient.

"So." Cade taps a stack of papers against the desk, straightening them. "We have our update on the conservatorship to submit to the judge. Here's what we're handing in, Zander."

Shock lifts my eyes to his and then back down to the report.

He pushes the papers toward me. It's a slim file. There is no legal reason I should see this right now. That anxiousness increases tenfold thinking there must be something damaging, something my brother is letting me see ahead of time to save our personal relationship.

I'm silent as I page through it carefully. When it came to Ella, I let my emotions get the better of me. I acted recklessly, but I'm not going to do it now.

I read the cover sheet, the second page, the third and so forth. Then I flip back to the beginning and read it again. All the while the men watch silently. The clock ticks incessantly.

Then I look into Cade's eyes. "This report leaves out a few things."

It's an intense statement to make. At The Firm, we pride ourselves on our integrity. Clients can trust us not to misrepresent the situation. This report Cade handed me might not contain outright lies about her progress, but it does tell a different story from the full truth of the last few weeks.

"I didn't think some details were necessary to include." Cade's talking about the night they caught me with Ella. My expulsion is also not included in the update.

It doesn't say that I've been disciplined in any way.

The report doesn't capture my brother's disappointment in me or how shaken Damon was when he realized what I'd been doing. There's nothing about the two of us other than that there is now a personal relationship that is deemed appropriate by The Firm. *Appropriate.*

"What does this mean?" I question.

My brother takes in a steadying breath, his thumb tapping lightly. There's a seriousness about him but something else is there in his gaze. "You are no longer removed. That was a temporary status. You are back as a member of The Firm."

Once again, shock hits me. He pulls something out from under the table. It's my gun in its holster.

I look at him, then stare at the gun. It's only now that I'm able to admit to myself how much I wanted this. I didn't want to be kicked out of The Firm. I was willing to live the rest of my life with the loss of it if that's what I had to do to keep Ella. But I never wanted to be separated from my brother this way. From all my brothers. I never wanted to be on the outside like this.

I'm afraid it's too good to be true. I'm afraid to even reach for the gun.

"Are you sure?"

He nods, but then I look at the other guys one by one. "I don't want this to be a split decision," I tell them all. It's possible there was a vote and some people didn't agree.

"It was unanimous," Damon says, cracking a smile. "We had a long-ass meeting about it." His smile widens and he adds, "We all want you back."

I haven't been this relieved since I brought Ella back from the brink after her breakdown. I feel like I'm taking a real breath for the first time in days.

"Go ahead," Cade says.

This moment feels as important as the first day I signed on with The Firm.

I lift the gun carefully from the table, stand up, and put my holster back in its place. When I sit down, Cade is pushing something else across the table to me.

My ID.

Those are the only two things I needed.

"How's it feel?" Cade asks and for the first time all day, he grins at me, everything feeling lighter.

"It feels damn good," I answer him and the guys laugh. Each of them stands and claps me on my shoulder in turn.

"It's good to have you back," Silas says and then adds, "Not that we could have got rid of your ass anyway." That gets the room filled with laughter again.

The shock still hasn't left me as I sit there, the reality sinking in. I never dared to hope that it would turn out this way. In fact, I planned on the opposite happening. I was ready to spend the rest of my life missing this job and all that comes with it.

I slip my wallet into my back pocket, and I can't help feeling like this is a sign. Like this was meant to be. Ella's meant to be with me, and I'm meant to be with her. I'm also meant to work at The Firm. If the universe had a problem with that, there's no way I'd be back in.

Thank God I'm back in.

"Now, let's get down to business," Cade says and the atmosphere turns more serious. The guys retake their seats and I already know where this is going.

Cade drums his fingertips on the table, returning to his usual brisk personality. "We've seen some things with these ... elite circles." He looks around at all of us.

"Any disagreement with my read on that?"

Damon shakes his head. "No." Silas leans back, his arms crossed and shakes his head too.

Cade returns his gaze to mine. "Ella was into some of it. Somebody is blackmailing her."

My blood turns cold. "Does Kamden know?"

My brother nods once and says, "I filled him in last night. He said he's almost certain he knows who it is and will trace it back."

"Does Ella?"

"No."

"Is he going to tell her?"

My brother stills. "We have asked that he doesn't say anything to her at this time."

I nod in agreement. "She's doing well. Very well. She's happy. There's no reason to alarm her if we can take care of this."

"That's what we suggested to Kamden. He agreed to give us a deadline before he takes things into his own hands."

I swallow the ball of anger in my throat. "What do they have on her?"

"Video," Cade answers, his tone solemn.

Shit. Video's the worst kind of evidence. It can be faked or manipulated, but most people don't have the necessary skills or technology. Video is usually trustworthy, and that's what makes it so dangerous. Even if it's fake, you can still be fucked over. People believe what they see more so than any other kind of evidence.

"Is it credible?" I ask.

"From what I can tell, yes," my brother confirms. "Kamden agrees. That's why he believes he knows who may have sent it."

"How much?"

"Two million."

"The hell's in it?" I ask.

Cleaning up messes like this is a specialty of The Firm's. We help people get out of impossible situations. I'm so glad they let me back in. If I hadn't known about this, Ella would have been at even more risk.

I wouldn't have been able to protect her from the various threats in her life.

If my brother had kept me in the dark ...

It would have torn apart our relationship. These are things I need to know. I remind myself again that it's all right. I *am* back in The Firm, and Cade did tell me. I have what I need to keep Ella safe.

Cade watches me from across the table. I don't know what I was thinking before. Cade would have told me about this even if I wasn't working for The Firm.

"What's on the video?" I press and take a look around the room.

"It's a video of her parents." His tone is sober. "Family secrets. And some truly fucked-up abuse."

I sit back and take it in. "Is Ella in the videos?"

"No," he says. "Not as far as I know, but that could change as we find out more."

I have to take a minute to sit with that. Fucked-up abuse scars a person. Ella seems focused on James's death as the cause of her spiraling, but clearly her trauma began earlier. It wasn't a single moment that triggered her downfall. A chill runs down my spine as I'm reminded of what Kam said at the house. *That she had a difficult life.*

This must have been what he was talking about. That's why he was drunk last night.

"What exactly is in the video? Did Kam see it?"

"Yeah. And he recognized it. He said it's not the first time the video has been used as blackmail."

"Did they pay last time?"

"Kam said the problem dissolved itself."

"What the hell does that mean?" I ask even though I know. Cade shares a look with Silas and Damon looks down to the floor.

"The problem went away on its own and I believe it was buried ten feet under."

Fuck.

"So it can't be the same person?"

He shakes his head slowly.

My jailbird.

I want to be with her right now. I fight off a strong urge to get up and leave the table.

But as much as I want to hold her, I want to keep her safe even more. That starts here and now, at this table, with The Firm.

"Okay." I look Cade in the eyes. "Let's figure this out. Ella is depending on us."

Chapter 12

Ella

The phone is clunky and old, but it does the trick.

I text Kam once I'm finished. **You know I could open apps on the laptop too right?**

Kam: Do I need to tell Zander to take it away?

I narrow my eyes at the old phone that's practically a brick.

Ella: No need. I don't have my passwords. I hope that eases his worries, but judging by what he says next, I'm not sure I accomplished that task.

Kam: No new accounts.

My eyes roll without my conscious consent.

Ella: I'm aware, Kam. I was just messing with you.

I debate on calling him to voice my discontent at not

being able to send a GIF of a dog rolling his eyes, but I decide not to since he should be here soon and I can tell him face-to-face.

Life is slowly going back to what used to be normal.

Well, other than replacing what used to be and rearranging finances. Kam is taking care of that, though. In less than a week three homes have gone into escrow, all cash. I try not to think of it and instead I scroll, searching for new properties and wondering if we should sell this one.

The fall breeze blows in through the cracked windows of the downstairs office, bringing in with it the faint smells of the season. The crisp autumn has always felt like home in some ways.

The cool air wraps around my shoulders as I sink deeper into the corner of the sofa with my laptop balanced on a throw pillow. I have to readjust so I'm not sitting on my flannel button-down top. Paired with faded light blue jeans, the outfit is one of my favorites for fall.

Not quite chic or uptown, but Zander said he liked it this morning.

I peek up through the doorway, knowing he's in the sitting room with Cade going over details I don't want or need to be privy to. He looked cute today too. In just blue jeans and a worn black tee. It amazes me how expensive and authoritative he appears, even in the simplest blue-collar attire.

My focus returns to the screen in front of me as I scan a listing in Miami and then email the link to Kam. Smirking, I can already hear him joking about retiring in Florida.

We could retire if we wanted. We could start completely fresh, just me and Z. We could hide away and go off the grid if we wanted. We can do whatever we want.

Or we could continue maintaining the status quo. I would be content with that. Although part of me thinks it's all just a fantasy and that once The Firm is gone, Zander will leave too.

I click over my tab to the email with The Firm suggesting to the judge that another psych eval be done. One to determine my competency. And for another doctor to be brought in once their term has ended, someone who will take over with my care plan.

It's odd to read it, this plan and schedule for a potential release of conservatorship. There's a fear there too, wondering if everything will be okay once they're gone. At that thought, I know it will be, so long as I still have Z.

Instinctively, I click over to another tab and read the tabloids with a Cheshire cat grin. Biting down on my bottom lip to keep my giddiness contained, I read the article again.

There's the mention of a possible baby and rumors swirling in the comments. All because of a hand on my stomach in one picture snapped. There's nothing to that rumor but it brings up all the hopes I had with James.

We wanted a baby. Once we finally settled down, we both wanted a baby. And now that will never happen. When I was in my late teens and twenties, the idea of an infant gave me hives. How could I possibly be a mother when I can hardly care for myself?

Now, even knowing how lacking I am, I know I would love a baby. I would give that baby the world. When we bought this house, we'd planned to start a family here, knowing there'd be plenty of room to expand. That was what sealed the deal for us. Now everything has changed and it's so empty here.

Tormented emotions swirl deep in the pit of my stomach and I have to close the laptop, swallowing thickly and reminding myself that it's okay. The front door opens and closes, and the sound of it makes me pull myself together.

That was the past, and now I have the future to look forward to. Clearing my throat, I set the laptop to the side and do what I can to shake off the heavy feelings.

I have no idea if Zander even wants a child or what he would think of having a baby with me. Or whether I should. The last thing I want is for a child to be brought up in this world as fucked up as me.

"That's not what was agreed upon." Cade's voice is harsh and it echoes down the hall. The cracked door carries the heavy footsteps of him leaving and a remark from Kam that I can barely hear. I'm slow to move, and quiet as I can be, attempting to eavesdrop on what appears to be a tense conversation.

With the footsteps getting closer, I stay perfectly still by the door. Cade's shadow passes and I peek through to see his back as he goes out the back way.

The sliding door is faintly heard over my rapidly beating heart as I listen to Z and Kam argue.

Something about money. Something about a note.

A chill sends pricks down my arm and I move without thinking. Numbly I make my way to them in the sitting room. I only hesitate outside the door for a moment. It's the statement "I don't know if we should tell her" spoken from Zander that has me pushing the door open. The hinges creak, announcing my arrival in an eerie manner.

Both of them stand, Kam in a sharp suit and Zander just how I saw him last in laid-back attire.

"Ella." Kam greets me as warmly as he can, but his grim look is telling.

"What's going on?" My tone is even and I should be proud of that fact, but looking up at Zander I feel considerably less than proud. I'm an intruder in a conversation he obviously doesn't want me to hear.

"Nothing to worry about. Just give us a minute, please."

My cheeks heat with embarrassment and there's a dull thud in my chest.

"I thought I heard my name," I comment weakly.

"Zander is learning some things," Kam comments condescendingly, his gaze fixed on Zander although he's talking to me.

"What things?" I question and Z responds to Kam rather than me, "She doesn't need to know." His voice is calm, much more so than before, and sympathetic.

With a half step forward, I refuse to leave and let them discuss me without being able to speak for myself.

"She knows more than you ever will," Kam says. His eyes flash to mine and there's a pain there I wish I hadn't seen. He swallows thickly before picking up his jacket and slipping it on. "I'll let you decide what you'd like to do."

With that he leaves. Barely squeezing my shoulder, quickly kissing my cheek and heading out without stopping when I ask him not to leave.

So many memories return. All of the times James and Kam got into it. There were a number of tense conversations and all for good reason.

But this?

"What happened?" I question Z the moment I can

and pinching the bridge of his nose, he asks me to stop. To let it be so he can figure it out.

It's hardly placating and I'm quick to open my phone.

"Who are you calling?" he questions and I answer "no one," turning my back to him and telling him he can have his minute. I'm quick to make my way back to the office and text Kam.

Ella: Talk to me.

There's the sound of a muffled bang from the sitting room and I'm vaguely aware of Cade coming back inside. Frustration echoes down the corridor and I can't ignore it.

Betrayal and anxiousness run thick in my blood.

I text Kam again.

Ella: What happened?

When he doesn't reply right away, I text him for a third time.

Ella: I'm begging, Kam. Please, what happened?

Kam finally answers and it doesn't ease a damn thing.

Kam: You should probably talk to Zander before me.
Ella: Are you sure?

My heart races, not knowing if Z will even tell me. I look down the hall and I can barely hear him talking to his brother, but their voices are far too hushed to hear a thing. Cade won't tell me what's going on, I'm certain of that.

The phone pings.

Kam: I'm sure. Ask him to tell you.

As the conversation continues, my worries intensify. My first question is the one most obvious to ask.

Ella: Is it something like ... like that would have made James mad?

His answer makes my blood run cold.

Kam: Yes.

Ella: Something Z did?

Kam: No. Z didn't do this.

Ella: Can't you just tell me?

Kam: Is that the way you want it to go? Or do you want to ask him to tell you?

Chapter 13

Zander

Ella faces off against me, her phone in her hands, her cheeks pink with emotion. I fucked up. I know that. We shouldn't have spoken about Ella when there was any chance she could hear. I can feel her slipping and it's a first for us since her breakdown.

It won't be the last.

Ella taps out one more message on her phone, then lets out a frustrated sigh. "You could tell me what it's about at least," she murmurs, peeking up at me, her head down, but her shoulders squared.

"Boundaries, jailbird."

"You need to tell me what you were talking about. It's not okay for you two to decide that you're going to keep things from me. How is that fair?" The leather chair in the office groans under her weight as she sits down, only to immediately stand back up. She paces as she types out another message.

Kam better not fucking tell her. "That's not what's happening," I say, attempting to reassure her.

"Isn't it?" She holds up her phone so I can see the text from Kamden on the screen.

Kam: Is that the way you want it to go? Or do you want to ask him to tell you?

"He won't tell me. Kam apparently thinks I should ask you, so that's what I'm doing. What were you talking about?" she asks.

Good. Knowing that Kam isn't going to put this knowledge on her is a relief, but I keep my expression neutral.

"We will take care of it." This is as much a test for her as it is for me. She gives me the burden, and I bury it for her. A chill runs down my spine, knowing that's exactly how Kam handled it last time. Or at least that's what he implied.

"I don't want you two to take care of all my problems and not even tell me about them." Ella shakes her head, her long hair swishing around her shoulders. Swallowing thickly, she says, "I should know."

"Ella," I say and her name is a warning.

"You just have to tell me," she says, her tone pleading.

Defiant. All I can think right now is that she's being defiant and this will play out one of two ways. I give her nothing but silence.

With a frustrated sigh, Ella pushes past me. I follow quietly behind her, deciding how exactly to handle this. To handle her. She moves quickly through the house and to the kitchen, where she opens one cupboard, then the next. A box of tea appears in her hand and she puts it down hard on the countertop.

"Ella, stop."

"I'm having tea," she says, her voice high and strained. "That's all I'm doing. If you won't talk to me, then I'm going to sit down and have a cup of tea." The water rushes down as she fills the kettle. Once it's filled, she turns it off with pent-up anger and adds, "Is there a problem with that?"

I cross to her in two steps and take her chin in my hand. The kettle lands hard on the counter and her shocked eyes look up at me.

Her chest rises and falls quickly. She's going to break down in a few minutes if I don't stop this, and I *will* stop this. Ella doesn't need to be swept up in fear.

It's just that now isn't the time to tell her.

"Jailbird, I'm sorry you overheard our conversation. We should have had it elsewhere."

She lets out a shaky breath. "No, you should include me," she pleads.

"No." My voice is firm. "I'm not going to tell you at this moment."

"Is it bad?" she whispers and I tell her it's nothing I can't handle.

With her lips pressed in a thin line, she stares past me, not at all happy.

"I apologize for causing you fear and distress, but now's not the time for you and me to discuss the topic. You need to be reminded of the rules." I keep my voice quiet. "The way you're acting right now makes me think you're being purposely disobedient."

Those last two words do exactly what I'd like them to do.

A new flush comes to her cheeks. Telling Ella she's acting out deliberately is the same as telling her I'm going to punish her, and she loves to be punished. It reinforces our connection to one another and it's a healthy release for her. It would probably do her good.

She takes a deep breath and lets it out slowly. "I'm not disobeying, Z."

"Look at me." Her dark eyes move to mine and stay locked on me. "Good girl." I tuck her hair behind her ear and her eyelids go heavy at the simple touch. "We will discuss this in our next session. All right?"

"I would appreciate it if you didn't keep things from me," she says, her voice shaking. "I think you should put an end to all this and just tell me what I need to know."

No.

Instinctively I understand that speaking to her about it now would only make the situation more fraught. I don't have a plan for what to say, and talking about this with Ella requires serious consideration, not spontaneity. There is far too much on the line to leave things to chance. I will tell her when I know exactly how it will be handled and ended. That way she'll have nothing to concern herself with.

"I'm taking you to dinner." There. That's a decision. Move our venue. Give us both some time to reset and calm down.

Ella's expression falters. "I know that's not what you were talking to Kam about."

"No, jailbird, it wasn't. But I'm not ready to talk about it with you. And you're not ready to hear it."

"Z ..."

"Do you trust me?"

She bites her lip. "Yes."

"I know it's hard, jailbird, but you need to keep trusting me now."

"Well, it feels like you don't trust me. It feels like you're hiding something because you think I'm too fragile."

"That isn't the case." She tries to look down and away. "Ella. You are not weak. You're my submissive and I provide for you. This is what I want from you. Control in all things. I crave your burdens. Give them to me."

There's a shift. It's slight, but it's there. "But ..."

"Trust me."

I know what I'm asking from her, and it's not easy to give it. But if we're going to get through this, and we are going to get through this, we need to be able to sit in these uncomfortable spaces."

Ella gives a shallow nod.

I lean down and kiss her.

When our lips touch, it doesn't erase the tension. I can still feel it in her body. But on a physical level, there's no misunderstanding between us. It's her lips against mine and then her tongue against mine, both of us seeking the other. It makes me hot for her. Too hot.

I pull away slowly from the kiss. "Come on. Get your shoes."

Her brow furrows. "I'm not dressed to go out."

I smirk down at her. She looks beautiful even if only in a flannel button-down and a faded pair of jeans. "Then I'll wait. You can change and we'll go wherever you'd like, jailbird."

"You make me feel like a jailbird more now than I have in a very long time."

Tension fills the room again. All I want is to put all of this behind us. The tumultuous and terrible things she's experienced. The growing threat that I'll handle along with the rest of the team. I want her to have a life like any other person who isn't a client of The Firm. As close as a socialite like her can get, anyway.

I can almost see it. A life beyond secretive conversations and conservatorships. I can practically envision her, happy at my side for whatever life throws at us.

The silence goes on for a beat too long, as if Ella is going to argue with me. The expression on her face looks like she's on the verge of spiraling. Of getting caught up in the meaning of us and The Firm and why I call her *jailbird*.

"Are you mine, Ella?" There is no negotiation in my tone.

She seems to return to me. "Yes," she says.

I lean in close to her mouth and nip her bottom lip. "Yes, what?"

"Yes, sir."

No matter what's happening between us, there's always a dark twinkle in her eyes when she responds to me that way.

"You're always my fucking jailbird. Now go get changed."

Chapter 14

Ella

The tip of my black stiletto heel taps against the base of the table. The anxiousness is not quite leaving me. We've never been like this. At odds. Given the power dynamic between us, there isn't a damn thing in my favor.

I've never felt this kind of vulnerable with Z. An unsteady exhale leaves me as he places our drink orders and the waiter leaves us in the private back room to ourselves.

Three of the four walls are furnished with hundreds of bottles of wine. It's as if we're in the middle of a beautifully lit cellar, ready for a romantic dinner below a black iron chandelier designed to look like a classic candelabra.

The room itself is intimate and the smells of savory

seasoning and sweet wines stir my appetite, even with the nervousness of knowing Z is keeping something from me.

His strong hand settles on my thigh, his thumb running back and forth where the emerald silk velvet of my dress meets my bare skin. It's a simple designer dress with a deep V-neck and long sleeves, yet it ends mid-thigh. I haven't worn something that hugs my curves like this in a very long time, let alone something so decadently expensive. His black suit is custom tailored and high end.

To anyone peeking in, I'm certain we would appear to be a power couple. Especially given how he's acting as if there isn't a damn thing wrong.

It was a long and quiet drive, but that hand of his has barely left me. It's as if he thinks he can contain me so long as he has physical possession of me.

Truth be told, it is comforting and he's not entirely wrong. But my mind won't let go of it. The wheels in my head turn and every possible horrid scenario fills my mind.

"Settle, Ella," he murmurs. I'm half surprised Z ordered me wine, but that only adds to the racing thoughts. Is it because he intends on telling me something that he thinks I'll need alcohol to absorb?

No, no, that's the opposite. Damon made it clear

as did Zander, when my spirits are low, I should avoid alcohol. It can no longer be a coping mechanism. Not in any way.

I swallow thickly, turning my attention to the candles lit on the table. That means then, that he's not going to tell me whatever it is that's happened.

"Do you think I'm weak and that's why you can't tell me?" I ask him again. I know that must be why. He could still carry my burdens, even if he told me what they were.

"You are not weak. I will tell you once I've decided it will benefit you."

I nearly ask who he thinks he is to decide what is and isn't good for me and the audacity of that thought has me reaching for the prosecco. The sweet drink is chilled perfectly; the bubbles crisp and refreshing.

Thankfully, we're interrupted by a young waiter presenting the chef's specials and a list with the fish of the day.

My appetite comes and goes as I ruminate on the possibilities. With a gentle squeeze, Z comforts me and orders for me as well, but it's not enough.

Just as the waiter leaves us, one hand on his skinny dark red tie and the other holding the menus, I prepare to lay it all out for Z. To tell him with finality that I can't be left in the dark on issues that pertain to me.

My lips part and my shoulders square to face him, but not a word slips out. I'm caught in his heated gaze. Fire crackles there and my body is paralyzed from the look he gives me.

"I require your obedience," he tells me, his gaze dropping from mine to my lips. "You are struggling with that tonight," he adds and his hand is released from my thigh. Leaving a chill to settle where the contact has been every moment he's been able to rest it there since we left.

As he sips his drink, an Arnold Palmer, I watch him.

"I am struggling," I admit and gather my strength to make my demands, but again I'm cut off.

"You have no reason to," he tells me and unbuttons his jacket, slipping the expensive fabric off of his broad shoulders and turning his full attention to me. His scent, masculine and woodsy greets me as I stare back at him.

"I don't know that."

"I'm telling you that. You should not worry. Not about anything. I have it handled." He's firm in his resolve. The control in his tone grants me a sense of security but still, I hesitate.

As he clears his throat, the cords in his neck tighten, and his presence seems to command the air to bend to his will. The strength and authority I know this man to be capable of come back full force. Like a switch flipping. A deadly one that demands obedience.

"You will not ask any more questions. Is that understood?" he tells me and I want to agree. I know I need to; I desperately need to let it go.

My bottom lip wobbles and my gaze flicks from Z to the candlelight.

"You are better than this," he murmurs and it cuts me, deep and unforgivingly. "You need to listen to me." It's not meant to. His tone is gentle and coaxing, yet the weight of it is too heavy for me to carry.

"I listen," I object.

"I need you to trust me." He grips my chin, giving me the physical contact I long for, more so than I realized until he's staring deep in my eyes. "Trust me."

"I trust you," I confess and his hold on me drops.

"Do you?" he asks and his voice is testing. His tone is low and his dark eyes narrowed at me. There's a shift between us and it steals my breath along with every bit of my strength.

"I don't mean to—"

"Stop," he orders. He signals for silence and I'm quick to obey. He is my Dom. *My everything.* Swallowing thickly, I nod. It feels as though I'm a child in trouble. Worse than that, I feel like I'm on the verge of losing anything and everything that matters to me. All because of his disappointment. How does he have such a hold on me?

Insecurity runs rampant through me as I twist the napkin in my lap. The chill across my skin is quickly heated when Z reaches out, his thumb resting on my bottom lip and a heat sparking in his eyes. "You are my good girl, Ella. You're going to listen to me now, aren't you?"

Nodding eagerly, I'm desperate to just go back to a few moments ago. I don't want to push him. I don't want to lose him.

As if reading my mind, he leans forward, kissing the crook of my neck and then whispers at the shell of my ear, "I am here for you, Ella. My very existence is for you. You have me, you will lean on me tonight and in every way I tell you to." His words send a warmth through me, a comforting security I desperately need. "Won't you, my little bird? You'll let me take care of you in every way, even if it pushes your boundary ... you haven't said your safe word. Have you even thought of it?"

No. His statement resonates deep within me. The safe word never entered my mind.

My heart races at the sound of the private door opening and Z pulls back, appearing completely unaffected. As if he didn't just have my entire world in his hand to do with as he pleased.

"And for you, miss," the waiter says, setting down the plate of perfectly seared scallops. "To start," he adds and asks if I'd like fresh ground pepper. He holds the pepper mill in offering and I answer "No, thank you" as politely as I can, attempting to contain myself and hold back the intensity that's been building since I took my seat in the burgundy leather dining chair.

Before the waiter leaves, I notice Zander pass him something that appears to be cash.

"What was that?" I question as soon as we're alone.

"A note to stay the fuck out for the next twenty minutes," Z answers as he pushes back the chair, towering over me as he unbuttons his shirt.

"Z," I protest breathlessly as he lays his shirt over the back of his chair and then pulls mine out, turning it with a commanding force and dropping to his knees in front of me. A thrilling shock takes hold of me. "What are you doing?" I barely manage to whisper as my blood heats.

"I don't want to dirty the shirt." He stares into my eyes. "I've decided I'll start my meal with your cunt," he tells me and my cheeks flare with heat that starts at my chest before bringing a warm flush all the way to my temples.

With his hands on the inside of my thighs, he spreads my legs, forcing the green velvet fabric to rise up.

A gasp leaves me as he grips my hips and pulls me to the edge of the chair. To keep my balance, I grip his shoulders, his bare skin hot under my touch.

"These need to come off," he says and slips the lace

down my thighs, leaving openmouthed kisses as he goes. His name escapes my lips amid heavy breaths of disbelief.

"You'll be quiet," he tells me in between kisses and when I agree, he licks my entrance all the way up to my clit. My back bows from the sudden touch and pleasure races through me.

My head falls back as he sucks and licks, toying with me and my sharp nails dig into his shoulders. I can't help but moan and the moment I do, he stops to grab the cloth napkin and brings it to my lips.

"Do I need to gag you?"

"No," I'm quick to answer and eager for him to continue.

"If you can't be quiet, I'll be forced to stop. Is that what you want?"

"No, I'm sorry."

"I know you are, but more than that, you're mine. Are you?"

"Yes." The single word is desperate.

"And you know I'll take care of you and that you should listen to me. You should trust me."

"Yes." My heart pounds desperately as he stares back at me, waiting for my submission. I've never wanted to give it to him more.

I reach out to him, my body moving of its own accord. I can barely push the words out when I say, "I trust you,

Z. I can't—" I have to pause to swallow. Closing my eyes as I do and when I open them, Z stares back at me with a raw intensity that seems to see through me. Through everything surface level and deep down.

"I can't feel like we're not okay ... I'm sorry and it's—"

"We are better than okay, Ella. You will always be mine. Even if you push me and fight. Even if you're disobedient. Even if you want more than I can give you for the moment." He kisses my wrist, keeping his eyes on me. "I will satisfy you another way and you will forget all about whatever it is that made you feel like we weren't okay."

A moment passes that crackles between us before he asks, "Understood?"

"Yes."

"Who do you belong to, Ella?"

"You, sir," I answer in a whisper.

I love you is on the tip of my tongue, but the words are silenced by his next command.

"Put your legs over my shoulders and enjoy what I do to you."

I nod in obedience and Z doesn't just eat me out, sucking and licking every inch of my heat until I come hard on his tongue. Once he's had his fill of that, he bends me over the table and fucks me so hard, I swear the table will break. It turns out, he did need to gag me.

Chapter 15

Zander

The Firm's offices have a completely different energy now that we're in prep mode for the event this weekend. Cade sits at the head of the table, file folders and a tablet in front of him. He scrolls through the information on the screen, his expression serious.

"Did Kam confirm his suspicions?" he asks, looking at me.

"On the sender of the letter?"

Cade nods. Damon slides a piece of paper over to him, and Cade glances at it before flipping it onto another stack within reach.

"Yeah. It's him. The same conclusion we came to." I can't even speak about these latest developments without anger churning in my gut. We matched a thumbprint but it's Kam who knew immediately. He knew who would have access and motive. There's no way I'm ever telling Ella a damn thing about any of this. No one should go through what she went through. "And the event Ella's friend is throwing is where he expects the drop-off."

Cade cracks open a dossier acquired on the suspect Kam has led us to. I've read it a hundred times over. It's him. The vile fuck has a name and it's at the top of my hit list. It takes everything in me to remain calm.

"Ah." Cade nods. "So that's why you're so inclined to go to a fashion show opening?" There's a hint of a joke in his tone that somewhat lightens the mood.

Hell yes it is. "That's right. Kam agrees it would be good to place her there as well. For PR, for us and also to address the situation person-to-person."

The humor fades from Cade's expression. "He's not going to see her, correct?"

"There are two hundred people expected to be at the event, including the press. We'll keep her away," Dane answers for me. Thank God he did. Just the thought that he would be near her makes my skin crawl.

I have to remind myself that he isn't the one who did those things. But to threaten her with that information … it's incomprehensible.

"So he will be at the event and we will confront him as we've done in the past." Cade switches off the screen of the tablet and looks first to Dane and Silas, then to me. "Are we prepared with ammunition of our own?"

Blackmail the blackmailer. "What we have on him is far worse and with one click, the police will be informed of everything. The blackmail and his other misdealings." Again, Dane answers. This isn't the first time we've handled these issues delicately. The police are never informed and the individual goes away quietly, not willing to risk us destroying their lives. I, however, wouldn't mind simply pulling the trigger.

"Has Ella been informed?" Cade asks.

Now the anger is replaced by worry. "No. She has no idea."

Cade exchanges a look with Damon. Heat coats the back of my neck at the thought of her finding out what happened. "How has she been in your sessions?"

Damon answers easily, "She's working through some things. Much more stable than she was when we took the case. Ella has shown a lot of progress when it comes to processing her feelings instead of letting them turn harmful. There is no question of her mental capacity. I feel confident signing off for the judge and ending her conservatorship."

"So long as the event goes accordingly. She needs

to show stability there, not just in counseling sessions," my brother comments and the thin skin around my knuckles turns white as I ball a fist.

"She'll be fine," I add, talking over Damon who then agrees with me.

My brother picks up a pen and jots down a note on a sheet of paper. Once again he glances at me. "Are you sure *you* can handle this?"

"I have no doubt."

I'm absolutely confident that with me by her side, Ella will make it successfully through the event without it throwing her into a spiral. I'm even confident that she can do it by herself. Damon has observed her work as far as her mental health, but I know that her inner strength is far deeper than he can imagine.

It's me I'm more worried about.

I'm not just pissed. I'm furious. A threat against Ella feels like a threat against my heart. I want to kill this bastard. How dare he threaten her? And with that of all things?

The video he sent makes me sick to think about. I watched it because, as a member of The Firm, I need to have all the information available to me. I wish it hadn't been necessary.

The video was of her father, along with a group of men. All of them were with a much younger Ella. There was a side-by-side comparison of what they'd done years before with her mother.

Rage heats every inch of me and I have to readjust in my seat, unable to keep still.

If there was any doubt that he was abusive, the tape was evidence enough. It wasn't a very long video, but it was long enough to know exactly what was going on.

"Any word from Kam?" Cade questions.

I take a deep breath and push the memories of that tape, along with my anger, down to a level where they won't damage my professionalism. "Kam said that this isn't the first time he's pulled this kind of behavior."

"So it's not the first time Ella has dealt with blackmail," Damon adds thoughtfully.

She's fragile, though. Strong. So damn strong. But fragile. I know Ella could get through this alone if she had to, but she shouldn't have to. "Kam's pretty adamant that he should handle the situation himself but I assured him we've done this before."

"You don't think he'll push back? Like he and Ella did last time there was a disagreement?"

My muscles stiffen, knowing he's referring to Kam's threats to destroy The Firm's reputation … because of me.

"No. He won't."

"What changed?" Cade looks me in the eye. "You had some doubts the last time we dealt with a situation involving Ella and Kam."

"I was unsure of where we stood as a couple last time. Now I know. And Kam is aware of that too."

The other guys shuffle in their seats. It's like they can sense my confidence about this. I'm not sure whether they're having doubts now or if it's something else.

"And where is that?" Cade asks, voice calm.

"She's still figuring a lot of things out, like Damon said." He was truthful in his assessment. And I trust his opinion on Ella's status too. There's a reason we're close friends. We wouldn't be if I didn't trust him. "As long as she'll have me, I want her. In all ways."

Cade glances at Damon, who gives him a subtle nod.

"You think it's going to last?" my brother questions.

"I know it is. She needs me, and I need her."

A frown briefly crosses his face. "Zander, she might not always need—"

I put my hand on the desk, cutting off his words. "Yes, she will. She needs someone like me and wants someone like me. Even if I wasn't brought up in the same circles as she was. I'll manage, and I'll fit in. Enough to get the job done. Enough to be ... enough for her."

Damon gives me an asymmetric smile from his side of the table.

Cade leans back in his seat, putting both hands ahead of him. "All right, all right. You can get off your soapbox.

I hear you."

"*We* hear you," Damon says, leaning forward and glancing around at all the other guys. "And it's about damn time. Next question. Should we tell Ella what's going on?"

"She doesn't need the stress." Nobody should have that kind of pressure hanging over their head from some sick prick, but especially not Ella. It's not her responsibility to protect herself from the guy, anyway. It's ours. *It's mine.* And that includes the planning.

"Are you sure?" Cade looks skeptical. "It might be triggering for her. But isn't it better to prepare her in case something happens? Damon, what do you think?"

My best friend looks at me, as if he's weighing what I'll think as well. He might take me into consideration, but I know he won't change his opinion to placate me. He'll say what he thinks, even if I disagree.

"I think transparency is always best."

Cade drums his fingers on the tabletop. "Kam said to let him handle it. Maybe we should listen to him."

It's a struggle. I want to have control over everything I can when it comes to the event. Yet I also understand that some things will be out of control no matter what I do.

"What are you thinking, Zander?" Cade asks.

"Yeah. You've clearly got some issues. Tell us what

it is," Silas says.

The problem, I realize, is that I started hiding things when I got involved with Ella. I felt secretive about it, and that extended to my own feelings about things with The Firm.

I can't operate like that anymore. Part of being back on staff is being open with them. We can't protect Ella effectively unless we're honest with each other. We can't protect any client effectively unless we're truthful.

"I'm frustrated," I admit. "My emotions shouldn't control how we proceed with the next steps, but if this guy was dead ..." My fists clench on the table. "If he was dead, there wouldn't be an issue."

"I agree with that," Damon says. "It's the son of one of the men in the video. Everything would be a lot less complicated if none of those guys had ever existed."

Cade muses out loud, "Are we certain she should attend? I understand it's best for the alibi and a public confrontation. But she doesn't have to be there."

All eyes are on me.

I sit in silence for a few more beats, thinking. "She's going and I'll tell her about the party. That will make her happy," I tell the guys. "It will add more substance to our report for the judge and I'm sure Damon would feel more confident in his assessment if she does as well as he thinks she will in a public setting with press and social pressure."

"It's not about making her happy," Cade says. "But—"

I cut him off. "It's about protecting her. I'm very fucking aware of that."

What Cade might not be able to understand, is that keeping Ella happy is part of protecting her. Of course her physical safety is always going to be a top priority for me.

But physical safety isn't the be-all and end-all. Her heart needs happiness, too, and letting her know about this party will give her a spark of joy. After all she's been through, she deserves it.

A life without happiness isn't a life at all.

"We're all going to go to that event and put an end to this." It's the beginning of the end for so many things for Ella.

Chapter 16

Ella

"I give up" is meant as a statement of weakness or exasperation. Or at least I always thought that's what it meant and that you were less than if you "gave up."

But releasing control and worries, giving them to Z… giving up has never felt so freeing. With James, he let me lean on him, he didn't take control. He didn't consume the burden and leave me free to just … be. I loved him so very much for being my partner.

Zander is more than just my partner, though. So very much more.

I've decided to let him handle anything and everything he wishes. The moment that switch was made, everything fell into place far too easily. It's almost too good to be true. Between Zander and Kam there isn't a worry in the world other than pleasing Z. Which is exactly what he commands.

My cheeks are sore and my lips are slightly swollen as my knees rub against the carpet.

"Do you think you've pleased me?" he asks in a husky whisper. Zander's voice alone sends shivers along my naked skin. I love the timbre of it, the deep need laced in between his masculine and controlling tone. He needs me just as much as I need him. He needs to take care of me as much as I need it. It's all simply too good to be true.

I murmur around his cock, humming that I have pleased him before peeking up at him through my thick lashes. He's naked, every inch of him. Dim light that peeks through the curtains from the moon outside slips across his hard muscle and deep grooves. He's a sex god, a greedy Adonis who's left me sore and satisfied and eager to do anything and everything he wishes.

I've *pleased* him for three days straight since the restaurant incident. Which I would very much like to do again.

I lean back to rest on my legs which are folded underneath me, the heels of my feet digging into my bare and reddened ass to catch my breath. I keep my balance, gripping his muscular thigh with my left hand

and stroke him with my right.

His hand spears through the hair at the back of my head and he tightens a fist around it, forcing me to look up at him.

He stares down at me with longing, and all I can hear is my racing heart. I don't deserve him, but I'll do whatever I can to keep him.

"How do you want me?" I question coyly and in an instant, his lips crash against mine with a hunger that I thought long ago would have waned.

If anything, the closer we get, the closer I want to be to him and it seems the same for him. *Please never leave me.*

"Just like that," he murmurs in a tone drenched with lust and tells me to put my hands on my thighs. "Tongue out and open wider," he tells me, nearly breathless with want. I do as commanded and watch him stroke himself, finding his release with a deep groan as he stares into my eyes.

His cum is warm and salty. "Swallow it," he commands and I do. Every bit of it.

As I shift from where I am, I can still feel him inside of me and the tender skin on my backside adds a hint of pain that only intensifies the pleasure.

He spanked me for mouthing off, fucked me until I came, and now this: finding his release in my mouth. It's the perfect fucking punishment, if I do say so myself. I watch as he gets dressed, putting on his dark gray pajama pants from earlier.

A smile plays at my lips as he lifts me gently and I cling to him until he carefully places me in bed with my tender backside up. I knew it was coming. It's routine now.

Even without the covers, without his touch on me, my entire body is lit with a warmth that stays with me all day and night.

It's a comfort and satisfaction that I desperately wish to hold on to.

He hums as his hand grips my ass and I respond immediately. My back arching, my bottom lip dropping. The sudden pleasure and pain were unexpected.

"You'll be quiet when I tell you to be next time won't you, little bird?"

"Yes," I answer immediately and he releases his grip, giving me a soothing rub instead. The cool gel I know all too well now soothes the heat the moment he rubs it in.

"I do love that mouth of yours," he growls as he rubs across my ass and upper thighs. I can't help the heat and the blush that comes over me. His praise is my drug.

I don't even remember what I said that led to a punishment. Probably something snarky and he bit back, so I bit harder. All I know is that he's far too aware, I was pushing just to push. Topping from the bottom is what he calls it.

"If tomorrow goes well, The Firm will issue a statement to the judge and all should go through easily enough."

"Kam told me the wheels were loosened," I confess to him, although I'm sure he already knows. He just may not know that Kam told me. I slip my arms beneath the pillow and peek back at him.

His shoulders rise and fall with a steadying breath. I realize he and Kam have differing opinions on what I should be privy to, but the two of them seem to have hashed things out from what I know.

Z's grunt, rough but barely heard, is telling. He doesn't like the manner in which Kam gets things done. Bribes and such. "The wheels are loosened, yes." His reluctance brings a smile to my lips that I try to hide in the crook of my arm.

The cool gel offers immediate relief and once he's done, he puts the cap back on and tucks it away back into the bedside drawer before climbing in bed with me. The mattress dips and groans with his weight as he climbs over me and then brings the comforter up around both of us.

I snuggle close to him as he wraps his arm around me. It's hard to believe this is real. That I could have another happily ever after, but that's exactly what it feels like.

"So you'll behave tomorrow in every way at your friend's opening. You won't push me, not even to play," he warns even though he doesn't have to. I'm acutely aware of everything that's at risk.

"I know," I tell him simply and then plant a kiss on his chest.

"Good girl." With his fingers under my chin, he tilts my head up to kiss me chastely. With his hand still there, his eyes searching mine, he tells me, "I got you something."

Surprised, I still, searching his eyes for what it could be. There's a mischievousness there and I love it.

He smirks. "You love gifts, don't you?"

"I do," I admit in a whisper and then sit upright on the bed, cross-legged with the blanket settled in my lap and not quite covering my breasts. My ass is still sore, but as he reaches into the bedside drawer, I can hardly pay the pain any mind. It's a good sting, one that adds to the residual pleasure.

A slim rectangular black box wrapped with a ribbon is revealed as he turns around. At first, I thought it was a ring maybe. I'm surprised by the disappointment that lingers for only a second.

"I thought you could wear it tomorrow," he tells me.

As I lean forward, he offers me the jewelry box. I pull at the red satin ribbon, letting it fall to the bed and open the gift.

A delicate rose gold chain lays in the box and hanging

from it, a woven diamond ring. The sparkling layers are entwined with rose gold shaped like flower petals.

"Z?"

"It's a promise ring and a collar," he tells me calmly but with something else there.

"A promise?"

"That I'm yours and you are mine, and I will take care of you, Ella. For as long as you will have me."

"That will be forever then," I answer quickly, teasingly almost but I can't hide the emotion that chokes me up. I'm quick to remove the chain and brush my hair back to put it on. It's long enough that the ring hangs low and rests between my breasts. I imagine the dress will cover it and I kind of like it that way. It's a promise the world won't see. Not unless I want them to.

"I'd like to get you one too, maybe?" I offer him as I slip the necklace around my neck. Z helps me when I struggle with the clasp.

He doesn't respond at first and my heart runs wild, wondering if he wouldn't want that. We've never talked about rings or marriage or children or any of that. And just as the insecurity sweeps in, he kisses the crook of my neck and his touch alleviates any and every doubt.

"I would like that very much," he murmurs at the shell of my ear and then pulls back just enough for me to be able to stare into his gorgeous hazel eyes. I want to ask him if tomorrow could be our first and last public outing. If we show the world our love and that I'm fine, and then we vanish. We give them just enough to leave us alone.

I want to say so much and make plans, but all of them jumble and I don't know how to say it right. I want him to myself. I want to be left alone with him. It doesn't sound right in my head, though, so I settle on a single truth instead.

"I love you," I confess. Unable to move or do anything else out of fear that this will all go away if I do.

"I love you, Ella. More than you know."

Chapter 17

Zander

"How are the nerves?" Damon asks as he adjusts his jacket.

"Still fucked," I admit to him under my breath.

"It's all going to go down as it's meant to," he assures me.

"I'll be calm once this is over."

Damon nods in agreement and then looks me up and down from where he stands in the threshold of the living room. "Well, at least you look like you've got your shit together."

I let out a huff of a laugh and gesture to my friend's cobalt blue suit that complements his dark brown skin. "You shape up nicely too. Trying to find a date tonight?"

I question with a smirk.

He smiles wide and broad, then says, "I think these women may be a little too high maintenance for me." He pats my shoulder and gives it a squeeze. "Tonight is going to be just fine. Everything is going to go according to plan."

I'm still nodding in agreement as he leaves me alone in the living room. The Firm is going first, scouting out the place and conducting reconnaissance. Silas stayed behind to drive us to the event once we've gotten the green light. I glance in the mirror again, making sure I look like the man who should be on Ella's arm tonight. I'm more dressed up than I have been in years. Tux. Tie. Everything. A spritz of cologne Ella picked out as well.

I've worn suits for The Firm just about every week for years, but this is another level. She's a socialite, or at least used to be. I could never imagine living with this constant pressure that comes with being in the spotlight twenty-four seven. If this is what she requires, I will be the man on her arm, the one leading her and standing by her side. Glancing toward the hall, I attempt to listen for her and hear nothing, so I check my watch one more time.

Whenever she happens to arrive, that is, I'll be the "man candy" on her arm, as Kam referred to my duty tonight. Releasing tension in my shoulders, I check the message from Kam, the one from Cade and as I do, my phone pings to let me know they're ready whenever we are.

Ella's been locked in her bedroom and the bathroom with a stylist for the last few hours, so I can't imagine how much longer she could possibly need. I spent as much time as I could getting myself ready, but there's just not that much for a man to do.

My clothes are on and I'm left with time to think.

I text them that I will inform them once we leave. As I hit send, the nerves amp up again.

Tonight is when everything changes. I hope, given all The Firm's planning, that we put an end to the blackmail threat quietly so we can provide everything Judge Martel requires without any hiccups. I want it all to be over by the time the sun rises. The conservatorship, the judge ruling in her favor, any and every threat. I'm ready to start our forever tonight. She's ready. I know she is.

Disastrous scenarios are possible, but I don't want to entertain them.

All of the unfortunate business will be behind us by morning.

I pace the living room of her house, trying to imagine a limit to the things I'd do for her. There really isn't one. I'd give her the entire world if I could. She accepted my collar, my ring.

She's mine. In every way and yet there's this lingering

warning. Tonight will end it all. I will end it all so she is only mine and there is no question about that fact. Not from her, not from a single soul.

Tomorrow she is mine, only mine and we start our forever.

Muffled voices get a little louder upstairs, distracting me. A woman laughs. One of the stylists, I think.

"Are you sure?" Ella asks after a door is opened, the sounds carrying down the staircase. I make my way toward the foyer to gather her for tonight.

"Yes," the woman answers. "Head on down. Do you need me to walk you?"

"Oh, no. I've got it. Thank you." As I make my way to her, the steady rhythm of her heels brings her closer to me.

Her stilettos click softly on each step and I go toward the sound. I'm drawn to her that way. I couldn't make myself stay away if I wanted to.

Before I've fully faced her, I'm paralyzed by the sight of her.

She takes my breath away. My bottom lip drops open slightly as I'm stunned by her beauty. Ella is gorgeous in a burgundy gown that skims the floor, carrying it with a grace that proves she was born to be dressed in silk. Her dark hair falls in soft curls. Her makeup is subtle and natural apart from deep red lips that match her dress.

The color brings out her beauty in a way I didn't know was possible.

She's so strikingly beautiful that my first thought is: I don't deserve her and I could never be the man worthy of being beside her. Until she speaks. "Z ..." Her gaze drifts down my body as she pauses on the bottom step and my heart races. "You look perfect. I love you in a tux, my God."

It's only then I can breathe. I lick my lower lip as I stare back at her and she blushes deeply. "You're breathtaking, my jailbird."

Her soft smile makes her that much more beautiful. I'm never going to see a more gorgeous woman. No one will ever be able to argue with me on that truth.

Ella finishes descending the staircase and meets me at the bottom where I'm quick to wrap my arm around her waist.

"I don't want to mess up your makeup," I say, "but I really need to kiss you."

"You won't mess it up." She lets out a quiet laugh. "They're professionals. It'll last no matter what happens tonight."

That comment makes my chest tighten with nerves that I'd forgotten about. "Nothing's going to happen tonight."

"No, of course it won't." Ella's eyes shine as she looks

me over once again. "I can't get over how good you look in a tux," she says softly.

"I'm nothing compared to you." With that I lean down and plant a kiss on her lips.

"Are we ready?" she asks.

I let myself look at her for one more long moment. This is the calm before the storm. Even if nothing goes wrong tonight, it'll be busy. Cameras and socializing and press. It's going to be the opposite of Ella's quiet house and the calm routines we've built up over her time with the Firm.

"Yes. Let's get you in the car."

Ella

Lights, camera, action.

There's a familiar buzz and thrill that lights through me, but also a tinge of fear. I remember my first appearance on a red carpet. I was fourteen and I had nothing to fear. Cameras flashed, I posed, I granted interviews to anyone who asked.

The first time I was labeled a socialite was two years later. At the party celebrating my sweet sixteen I arrived covered from head to toe in Chanel's new line that was released the week after. I was the "it" girl. Access to wealth beyond imagination and friends with anyone who was anyone ... because of who my father was and how many dollar signs were attached to my name.

Then at eighteen, after a sex tape scandal, all the hottest designers begged me to wear them. All I got was attention. Good and bad both. Kam took me under his wing when things got too heavy. "Any press is good press" is a lie when mental health is added to the mix.

The number of people who told me to kill myself after I was photographed with a director who was married was in the thousands. Rumors spread like wildfire. I posed because he asked. The man wasn't even my type but I was a homewrecker nonetheless.

And yet, with the onslaught of negativity, the lights never stopped flashing. The comments poured in and Kam made sure to fix it all. Putting out one fire after the next.

As Silas drives the car away and Z gives my hand a squeeze, I stand tall off to the right, knowing they're waiting. There's a banner and bright lights set up for the private fashion line reveal.

Martinis served on silver platters right after. I recognize half of the photographers and a reporter at the entrance. At least thirty people stand out front of the massive estate. The guests are waiting on the right side of the red velvet rope; photographers and press crowd the other side.

Trish told me the only reporter I'll be speaking with tonight has been paid off. Kam gave him a list of softball questions to ask so I won't be surprised or caught off guard. It's rigged, so to speak.

"You all right?" Z questions, soft and low. In the shadows beside the grand foyer, only feet from where the night will begin, I feel nothing but doubt.

I don't know if I can go through it all again. The highs are the best highs, but the lows ... the lows have almost killed me so many times and I don't know how many lives I have left, but I want this one. I want my happily ever after without this.

"We can go back to the house," he offers.

"No, no, just preparing myself," I tell him. Moving to my tiptoes in my heels, I plant a kiss on his lips.

The perfectly manicured lawn is split with a paved path that will lead us to the start of the event. A photo, a sound bite, a martini and then I can hide inside.

"Are Kam and Trish inside? Do you know?" I ask Z as a cool breeze comes by, much colder than I expected. Warmth is just around the corner.

"They are. Everyone is." Z then asks, "Do you want my jacket?" He's already removing his tux jacket and I have to stop him, grabbing the expensive fabric, pulling it back into position and tapping his chest.

"I'll just move quick so we're inside fast," I tell him and then take his hand. "Let's do this." I tug, but he doesn't move. Looking back, I find his gaze searching mine.

"We don't have to if you don't want to."

"I think tonight …" I trail off, then clear my throat and tell him what I've been thinking all last night and today. "I think tonight, I will show them that I'm all right and I prove that people can have second chances. And then I can walk away if I want, knowing I at least said goodbye in a way that makes me feel like I did what I needed to."

His brow furrows when he asks, "Is that what you want?"

Nodding repeatedly, I swallow the lump in my throat. This is the goodbye I want to leave them with. A pretty dress. A pretty smile. And telling the world how happy I am to be here. Even after everything that's happened, I want to tell them what a wonderful night it is to be alive.

"It is. I really have to do this." Another kiss and Z wraps a strong arm around my waist, kissing my bare shoulder and whispering, "Then let's get on with it, my little bird."

He leads the way and my heart rampages, the rapid thumps growing louder and louder in my ears as we get closer to the event.

"Ella!"

"Eleanor!"

The photographers call out my name and I face each of them with Z behind me and then at my side. The first snaps are posed. Then I grab Z by the tie, surprising him and kissing his cheek and then his lips while the bright lights flood the area.

"I wasn't expecting that," Z says and smirks, both of us very aware the cameras are still flashing.

All I offer him is a simper. They could photograph me kissing this man all night long if they wanted.

The calls of my name, the laughter and white noise—I've been here before, but it feels different now. It's broken, part of it like heaven and the other side hell.

"Eleanor, my love!" Charlie, the reporter Kam handpicked, motions for me and I escape to him, knowing there's a drink and sanctuary after this moment.

"Charlie." I greet him by reaching out and holding on to his left arm, the one not holding the mic. I give a half hug with a wide smile and there's a flash and then another as a paparazzo captures the moment. "I've missed you," I say, keeping my tone playful and my voice loud enough to be heard over the gaggle of people around us.

"Oh, not as much as I've missed you." We air-kiss

on each cheek as we've done since I was only a teenager before I release him and take a step back where Z gathers my arm around his.

"And this is your ..." Charlie questions immediately, getting right to the point and eyeing Zander.

"My knight in shining armor," I answer with a simper and then add, "Well, in Armani, but you know my tastes are little more grown up than fairy-tale stories."

Charlie laughs at my joke and I peek up to see Z smirking, handsome as hell and for a moment it all fades into the background. When I was a little girl, I dreamed of this. This very moment and yet all I want to do is steal away with him now.

"Do you have any exclusive details you could offer me?" Charlie questions with a raised brow, holding the microphone out for me. "Maybe?" He pushes forward and I debate for only a second.

"I think I may be in love," I tell him and then look back at Z to find him smiling down at me. I don't know if he's playing his part perfectly or if he just happens to be perfect.

"Oh my!" Charlie's eyes go wide and I laugh.

"Got to go, my love," I tell him and turn slightly to leave.

"Anything you can tell us about the launch tonight before you go?"

"It's going to be thrilling," I answer him and then

add, "This designer is to die for."

"Have a drink for me, Ella," Charlie calls out as I take two side steps toward the house.

I'm quick to reply with my normal response, "I'll have two!"

As Z leads me away, toward the front foyer where warmth is already pouring into the night, he whispers comically at the shell of my ear, "The hell you will," and I let out a genuine laugh.

The chandeliers are breathtaking in the dimly lit expansive space. Kelly's open floor plan has been rearranged and redesigned just for tonight. With a raised runway running through her living room, the floor-to-ceiling glass doors are all open, allowing the runway to end in her perfectly manicured backyard. Every piece of furniture is white, blending into the marble floors. The black runway provides a stark contrast that's truly stunning and half the guests are already seated, the other half chatting and drinking and laughing. Everyone is dressed in creams, golds and black.

Kelly shakes her hands out before accepting two martinis, garnished with olives, from a silver platter. The theme of tonight is *Sex and the City* chic and I am here for it. And somehow dressed appropriately.

"It's a great turnout," I tell her as I sneak up behind her, kissing her cheek.

"Ella, baby!" she squeals, passing the drinks back to the waiter dressed in a simple black suit and tie. He's young and handsome, more than likely a model hired for the evening.

"I should have had you model tonight," Kelly says with a pout. She looks me up and down, adding, "You look stunning."

"Well, thank you but that's a bit of the pot calling the kettle black," I reply with a knowing smile. She does a little twirl in her gold gown adorned with crystals.

"It's reminiscent of Marilyn," I comment and she lets out a girlish squeal with her lips pressed in a broad smile before telling me, "I know, right?"

"It's one of the designers?" Zander asks from beside me and it's only then that Trish sees him.

"Uh, yes, but also, damn Zander," she says, then pats his arm with a shocked but overwhelmingly impressed expression. "You clean up nice, Playboy."

He gives her an asymmetric grin and replies, "Thank you." His arm finds its way around my waist again and I lean into him just slightly.

Friends, fashion, drinks and celebration. I do love this part.

"Hold on," Kelly says, holding up a finger before pulling out her phone. She snaps a quick picture and as she does I see a few other guests, who I'm not familiar with, doing the same. "I have to send this to the hubby. He's on a business trip that I will never forgive him for."

She types away with a smirk, no doubt bragging about the party but also telling him how much she misses him. She's a romantic at heart.

"And this," she says, handing a drink to me, "is for you."

"Oh, I uh—" My hand raises slightly and Kelly moves forward before I can reject it completely. "Virgin, my dear," she whispers. Peeking up at Z, he nods.

"I can listen to orders too," Kelly comments and then laughs at her own joke.

I accept the martini glass and sip. All the while, Z watches.

"Good?" he questions and I nod.

It's refreshing and goes down easy. I don't know exactly what it is, but there isn't a hint of alcohol in it.

With a hand on either side of my waist Zander asks in a murmur if I like it and I tell him it's delicious.

"Good." He kisses me and then asks if I'll be all right for a moment here.

"Yes, but where are you going?" I question.

"I'll be back in just a moment. Stay where you are and don't leave," he commands.

"Z, is everything okay?" I ask although I keep my voice down. Kelly is keeping a watchful eye on me although she's currently handing out drinks to a pair of women passing behind us. Knowing she's occupied with them for a moment, I part my lips to question him further, but he stops me.

"There's nothing you need to worry about. I'm just meeting with the team for a moment. You'll be fine here. Or would you rather I stay?"

A moment passes and Kelly returns to my side.

"I'll be fine," I tell him. "Go." My heart does a pitter-patter watching him leave me after he kisses the back of my hand.

Kelly is unaware of the shift and claps against her martini glass, letting out an *aww*.

"He really is a knight in shining armor, isn't he?" she comments.

"That he is," I answer with a half-smile and sip the virgin drink once again.

"Ask for Ella's Snowball at the bar and you'll get one of these," Kelly informs me before looking past me and squealing with delight.

Her throat is going to be sore and her voice gone by the morning.

I half turn with the drink to my lips only to have the glass nearly taken away.

"Hold on now," Trish says and sips the drink, lifting her off-the-shoulder black chiffon gown with her left hand and holding the martini glass with the right. "Z told me no alcohol for you tonight and to help be your keeper."

I would laugh like Kelly does but instead I hush Trish. "Don't call him Z here—that's just for us. I don't want anyone to overhear."

There's a moment of contemplation in Trish's eyes, followed by a soft smile. "What?" I question.

"Nothing, just … just déjà vu. You know when you get that it's supposed to be a sign that you're in the exact place you're supposed to be."

The quiet reflective moment is over with the DJ requesting guests be seated in the next ten minutes for the show to start.

"Cheers, my loves," Kelly says as she hands Trish a drink and Trish hands mine back.

Our glasses clink and the lights dim further.

"We're needed up front," a man in a gray suit with a silver striped tie says over Kelly's shoulder. Kelly finishes her sip, and quickly introduces him to us before running off with him.

I vaguely recognize his name from some event a while back and I'm fairly sure the two of them had a fling back then. It's practically ancient history, though, since it was before Kelly got married.

"Good luck tonight," Trish says.

"You got this," I add and off Kelly goes, hand in hand, dressed to the nines with a French designer and the spotlights shifting to be on them.

Applause fills the room and I join in looking to my right and then my left, waiting for Zander to emerge.

"Do you want to take our seats?" Trish questions, already tugging on my arm.

"I want to wait here I think," I reply and again I look over my shoulder for Z. "He said he'd be right back."

"He might be a little bit," Trish comments and I stare back at her with my blood running cold.

"What do you mean by that?" My voice is deathly low as the designer takes the floor, announcing the new line and partnership with Kelly.

Trish searches my face seemingly confused before asking, "Did neither of them tell you?"

"Tell me what?"

She only gets a few hushed comments out before Zander is back at my side. Shivers climb up the back of my neck as I stand there, absorbing it all as quickly as possible so as not to show that I now know what he wanted kept from me. There's a pounding in my chest as he kisses my cheek like nothing's wrong and asks the two of us, "Could I walk you to your seats, ladies?"

A moment passes before a smile graces my lips and I

let him take my hand.

All the while, turmoil and fear rage inside.

Still, it's: Lights. Camera. Action.

Chapter 18

Zander

With adrenaline pounding through my veins, the last thing I want to do is leave Ella, even for a minute. I loosen the tie at my throat and make sure my presence won't be missed.

There's a round of applause as Kelly passes the microphone back to the MC and the lights dim even lower so the spotlight is only on the runway. Ella's hand hasn't left mine since we sat down. We're strategically placed in a private corner. It's easy to come and go.

Kamden thought of everything.

As I prepare to leave, Ella squeezes my hand and her dark eyes peer up at me.

I don't want to walk away from her side.

Unfortunately, it's necessary. This is part of the job. And it's my responsibility, as Ella's Dom and the man she loves, to ensure her safety. There's a flicker in my chest as she stares at me, as if she knows I'm leaving again.

I'm the man who loves her. Anything less than what I'm going to do tonight wouldn't live up to our relationship.

I lean closer to her, breathing her in before telling her, "You stay with Trish." I keep my voice low so that only she can hear, but I make sure she knows it's a command. "You'll stay right here, or accompany her if she needs. You will not drink alcohol, and you're going to keep your phone on."

My pulse hammers as I prepare to leave her. She will be fine and I won't be gone long.

A moment passes of silence as she stares back at me and then swallows, looking down before looking back at me. "You'll be fine, my jailbird. You'll be perfect even," I tell her, reassuring her and kissing her temple. "I'll only be gone for a moment and I'll be back before the show is over."

Ella looks deeply into my eyes. I can tell she's responding to my tone. Her face flushes, and a hint of worry comes to her expression, but she gives in, trusting me as she should.

"Yes, sir," she finally says. She leans in and kisses me.

Her lips brush against mine and I almost find myself lost in the moment.

This is the start of our forever and I'm going to destroy everything and anything that stands in the way of that. With one last squeeze of her hand, I leave her and give Trish a nod. As I pass through the back, Silas is there, hands clasped in front of him. He nods my way and I return it as we share a glance.

She is safe, I remind myself and quicken my pace.

As I make my way through the event space, I keep in mind that whatever happens tonight has to be done quietly. We cannot afford for the police to get involved. If they are, any chance of a judgment in her favor regarding her conservatorship is fucked.

No kinks, no hindrance. With the show starting, there's only a single waiter in the hall, and he doesn't see me as he heads to the kitchen. Apart from him, the hall is vacant. I turn the corner, knowing the meet is to take place by the garage. As I glance at my watch, movement ahead catches my attention.

Heat dances along the back of my neck as I spot Kam, slipping out of a side exit and into the side yard of the estate. He's not a member of The Firm and with the secrets he's kept, I don't know if I can trust him.

Moving quickly, I catch up with Kam. I track him to a staircase that winds up the corner of the event space.

He's just moving out of view when I begin to take the stairs behind him, keeping my footsteps as quiet as possible. I'm not sure how he'll react when he realizes I'm following him.

He's not supposed to be at the meet so I don't know what the fuck he's doing. Glancing at my watch again, it's nearly 9:30, the time of the drop. My heart hammers as another door opens and then closes with a creak. I rush to catch the heavy door before it shuts completely. If he hears it, he'll know someone's behind him.

Then again, it doesn't really matter. Kam's reaction isn't as important as what he knows.

He exits the stairs at the third floor and moves down the hall with long, confident strides. He knows exactly where he's going. This estate is a winding maze, but I'm certain he's been here a hundred times before or more. After all, Ella said the group of them have always been close and it's Kelly's home. Kam doesn't even look back as he approaches a door near the end of the hall, opens it, and goes inside.

Immediately, voices rise. I can't tell what they're saying but they aren't friendly tones.

Swallowing thickly, I steel myself and move slowly toward the door taking each step carefully, my hand on the butt of my gun. The door stands open and I position myself so that I can see inside.

I peer in through the threshold. It's a large office, one with an anteroom containing a silver bar cart holding bottles of wine and whiskey. The dark liquids are illuminated by the single light from a standing lamp. The small chamber leads to a bigger room with a heavy wooden desk and behind it, shelving with books and antiques. Judging by the stacks of boxes and rolled-up rug in the corner, I can't imagine anyone uses this office for any purpose other than storage. Shadows move about the room as the voice tells Kam he shouldn't have interfered.

Fuck. A dull click can be heard and it's then that I pull out my gun. *Fuck, fuck, fuck.* We need the team here.

What the hell is Kam thinking? Adrenaline races as I text Cade 911 and the intense situation escalates further with a round going off and the voice not belonging to Kam yelling out, "Fuck, man." The click is heard again and all I can gather is that Kam gave a warning shot before speaking clearly enough that there's no doubt when he says, "I told you that you would regret it if you didn't leave her alone."

"I'm sorry. Kam. It was a mistake. I take it back."

"You can't take back threats like that," Kam says although the words are muffled.

I ease in through the doorway, preparing for chaos. This wasn't the plan and all I know is that I have to get back to Ella. This needs to end now.

It happens fast, the second I turn the corner.

Kam raises a pistol with a silencer attached. I can't see his face, but I can tell from his posture that he's not unfamiliar with firing a gun or upset at all about doing it.

I glance at his target as my pulse races, a man I recognize from the dossier. He shakes his head, hands up, staring at Kam. He's dressed to impress as well in an expensive tux, and not much older than me. Kam says, "Once you're a threat, you're always a threat," and fires.

The bang is nearly inaudible but the gut-wrenching heave from the suspect is telling. The man looks down to what was once a perfectly pressed white button-down, quickly soaking up blood right in the center of his chest.

The man looks up at Kam, wordlessly dropping to his knees, then down flat.

A moment passes and then another as I stand there in shock. Ella's closest friend peers down at the body and waits a few beats before stalking to the body, checking to see if the man is alive.

Kam turns his head and looks right at me. "He's dead. You need to find the safe. The video's going to be in there and it needs to be destroyed." He holsters his gun. "The backup safety net's already been secured."

Backup safety net. I barely hear him. The shock of what I just witnessed is still sinking in.

For the first time all evening, and maybe in months,

I'm uncertain about my assumptions. Not so much at Kam's words, but his demeanor.

"You just killed a man in cold blood."

"It was him." Kam glances between the man and me. "We already confirmed it. You know that. His fingerprints were on the envelope. When I asked him how he wanted the money, he had the balls to smile and say, 'The security firm is taking care of it.'"

The body cooling on the floor is evidence that I underestimated Kam. No signs of life come from the corpse.

"You've done this before," I say to Kam, and the statement comes out flat.

"I didn't do this. You did this." It takes me a moment to register what he's said as he comes closer, passing me the gun he used. "Give me your gun," he demands and I only second-guess switching our weapons for a moment. My prints will be on a gun just used to kill a man, but as I look down between the one he's holding and the one I have in my possession, I know he used my gun. One registered to me.

"Fuck," I mutter.

I'd been holding this gun, one that's slightly different but not enough that I questioned it, down at my side, aimed at the floor. For a single moment I hesitate, but it passes. I'm already in this with him. We're in this together now.

With a chill settling down my spine, I swallow thickly before flipping over the gun and handing it to him.

"Don't worry," Kam says easily. "Your secret is safe with me."

I give a humorless laugh. "You set me up?"

He shakes his head and with that small motion plus the look he gives me, I feel a sense of ease. "I didn't. I brought you in. That's what I did. I brought you in on one condition."

"Brought me in?"

"In the circle with us. Like I said, on one condition."

"What the hell's that?"

A grin spreads across Kam's face. "You marry her. A whirlwind romance. Legal only, if you want. The marriage can exist only on paper if that's all you want it to be. I don't care. But you're going to marry her to protect you both."

I stare back at him, searching his expression for some clues on what the hell his reasoning is.

Kam gives me a sad smile. "If you don't want to marry her, you can leave. You're in or you're out, and either way, you're not going down for this." He gestures to the gun in my hand and adds, "That was just for insurance purposes, if you know what I mean."

"If I leave her, you tip off the cops?" I ask for

clarification.

"No," he corrects me. "If you *hurt* her, I destroy your fucking life."

We share a look of understanding before I nod, slipping the gun into the holster and telling him flatly, "We don't have any problems then, other than how we're going to cover this up and keep it from Ella so she doesn't get hurt."

"She knows it all, Zander."

A soft rustle in the hall draws my attention a second before Trish comes into the room. She crosses the anteroom with measured steps and glances down at the dead body. Then she looks at Kam. "Is everything okay now?" She's not at all afraid, only cautious.

"We still need the safe," Kam tells her. "The tape, specifically."

"I know where it is," Trish answers and then says, "I can take care of that."

It dawns on me, that murder isn't something that's unfamiliar to ... as he called it, the circle.

Heels click behind me, and Ella enters the room at the same time my phone buzzes and then buzzes again. I glance down to see my text never sent to Cade. He's sent me two messages in the meantime, though.

Cade: Where are you?

Cade: The exchange hasn't happened yet. We're

still waiting for him to arrive.

Dread washes over me, knowing this isn't over yet. "Z?" Ella whispers and Kam ignores her, unrolling the old carpet in the corner of the room. Trish has already left.

"Ella, don't—" I attempt to shield her, but what's done is done and there isn't much I can hide from her as she walks in.

I brace myself for her emotions to overwhelm her, but she only glances at the body and then back up to me.

"You could have told me. But it's okay you didn't."

"Kam," I start, not withholding my anger that he would go behind my back.

"Not me—" Kam answers from where he's crouched on the floor, hands in the air at the same time Ella tells me.

"Trish didn't know that I didn't know," she comments softly, again looking behind me. "She wouldn't tell me what he had"—she pales staring down at the lifeless man before looking back up at me—"but I know who he is so I'm pretty sure I know what you saw."

I swear I can feel her heart break at this moment. Tears prick her eyes as she stares up at me.

"You don't need to worry about that, my jailbird," I murmur, vaguely aware that Kam is listening. Gripping her chin between my fingers, I force her to look up at me.

"You still love me?" she asks, her hand reaching up

to the center of her chest and it dawns on me that the ring I gave her last night is there. Just beneath the deep red silk.

"Of course I still love you …" I trail off and take in a steadying breath, hating that there's any doubt at all from my Ella. "I don't want you involved in this and you should worry that you disobeyed me."

"I didn't," she says and perks up. "You said I could accompany Trish."

I'm speechless for a moment, staring down at her knowing she is once again topping from the bottom. "We'll discuss this later," I tell her and then kiss her gently. Then another kink in the chain dawns on me. "How did you get away from your security detail?"

"Silas?" she says and I nod, swallowing down the disappointment that she outsmarted the fuck out of me. "I left Silas by the powder room in the east wing on the first floor."

"Go now, back to him. And you will text me once you are back with him. You will say nothing at all about what happened and you will go back to your seat and wait for me, is that understood? No … going around my rules or loopholes."

My cunning, beautiful girl has the nerve to smirk at the last line. "Your ass will pay for that, Ella."

She bites down on her bottom lip and it slips out

easily as she murmurs, "Yes, sir."

"Kiss me," I command her and she does. As if there isn't a worry in the world.

"Now go." I send her off and she waves at Kam, telling him goodbye as well.

It's only when she's gone that I breathe out deeply, staring down at the unanswered messages from my brother and then to my left, to the dead body Kam has dragged onto the rug.

"Since I seem to be playing your game by your rules ... How do we cover this up?" I ask.

Kam's on his knees at the edge of the rug and I join him on the other side. "He lost a hell of a lot of money," Kam explains with a grunt as he rolls the body up in the rug while I help. "As of two hours ago, his wife left him because she discovered the mistress he's had on the side, along with the bank accounts being emptied. I'm guessing the cops are going to think he either ran off with the money to a remote island or killed himself."

He says it so nonchalantly.

I look down at the body, his lower half now wrapped in a rug. There's no way this guy could have killed himself like that.

"His body will be cremated by tomorrow." Kam stretches with his arms above his head, then cracks his neck. "You probably don't know how this works, Zander.

We decide what goes on paper. The coroner has already determined that he shot himself after receiving phone calls from both his wife and mistress. They both left him over the loss of millions of dollars in a single week. It's not uncommon."

I'm speechless. The ease with which the explanation leaves Kam's mouth is unfathomable.

The coroner hasn't decided anything. The coroner hasn't even seen the body. Yet Kam speaks like he knows it's a done deal. He watches me with tired eyes. This man isn't a ruthless killer, just a realist about the world Ella comes from. He said he would do whatever it took to protect her, and he meant it.

He doesn't do this for the adrenaline rush. There's a limit, and Kam has reached it, appearing far more battered than I've ever seen him.

"We're going to take care of one another," he tells me. "You understand?"

"I think so," I say.

"You need to know so. There's no going back. I don't enjoy this, Zander. I don't want this. But we do what we have to. You can understand that, can't you?"

"I can."

"Good, then marry her," he says. "Legally, at the very least. There needs to be that level of protection."

"What about my brother? What about The Firm?

They're waiting for me and for … him."

"Your brother and The Firm can never know the details. They can learn of his disappearance when it's reported in the papers."

That one hits differently. A chill runs through me as I glance down at the body, the rug now wrapped around it twice and firmly secured.

"I don't like lying to my brother."

"You have to," Kam says easily. As if he already knows I will go ahead with it.

I don't want to lie to Cade. I did it once before, and it ended up with me nearly getting kicked out of the goddamn group. And I don't like lying to the rest of the team.

But if this is what it takes, I'll do it. Anything for Ella.

I make the deal with Kam, finalizing tonight. "I'll keep this secret, so long as after tonight I can take her away from all this. Somewhere safe."

"Somewhere warm," he adds, seemingly agreeing with me. "I'd like to retire from this bullshit as well. You have a deal. Take her away, protect her. Provide for her. She'll always have a home here and that doesn't mean we're going away. But a bit of quiet will be good for her I think."

"So that's a deal."

"It's a deal," he says with finality.

Kam said he brought me in because we understood each other, and it turns out he's right. I'll do anything when it comes to her.

Even keep this secret.

The uncertainty still plagues me. Kam must see it in my expression as we stand together, a dead body at our feet. "I can tell you don't like this, keeping it from The Firm, but if they know, they're a threat. That means other people might come for them."

"I don't want to involve them," I admit.

"Good. Neither do I. Keep them safe. All men like us protect the ones we love. We keep the people around us safe, whether that means keeping a secret or ending a life. That's what we do."

Chapter 19

Ella

There are certain circles where the rules are different.

Where your mother can blackmail your father into marriage. Where he can then abuse her and their child when she's at the age of his friends' liking.

Where relationships are used as bargaining chips and money is more important than truth. Where lies can be spread and believed. Where palms can be greased and problems go away.

Those are the circles where murder is a way of life for those nasty moments that threaten to destroy you.

Kam was my savior when he helped get rid of my father, but he couldn't ease the pain that lingers from a life brought up like that. He would know.

I thought James was my escape and I was his. He was my happily ever after in a fucked-up fairy tale written with a diamond-crusted pen and passed around in dark corners of coke-fueled parties.

He took me away and showed me life could be different. And then fate caught up with me, that cruel bitch.

"He asked you to marry him?" Kelly asks, glancing down when I look back at her in confusion. I clear my throat and do everything I can to shake off the sudden emotion that's overwhelmed me.

"You keep fiddling with it," she comments.

Peering down, the rose gold ring still on its chain sits between my fingers.

"If you don't want people to know, you better slip that back in," Kelly warns and then takes a sip of her champagne.

The after-party is in full swing, the music so loud, the bass vibrates my chest. "Do you think anyone saw me—"

I don't have to finish. Kelly reassures me just like I've done for her a hundred times before. "No one, babe," she whispers and tells me she loves me. "You okay, though?"

"Just ... a lot," I answer her, not knowing if she's aware yet. I don't want to be the one to tell her.

She gives me a sad smile and takes a curl of mine in

her hand before setting it back into place. "If it means anything at all," Kelly tells me, "I think James would have liked him. Even if he's quiet and brooding, he's protective of you. You can tell and James would have liked that."

"Thanks," I murmur and return her smile.

When James died, I swore someone did it. An enemy saw to it.

But the evidence was on camera. It was only a tragedy.

He suffered my karma. All the reckless bad I'd done in my life ... and he was the one who suffered the consequences.

I thought I was okay seeing that man upstairs ... but the sight of him lying so still ... "I need Zander, I think."

"I'll cover for you, babe," Kelly tells me and kisses my cheek before striding back to her party.

I'm halfway across the room to my security detail dressed in a sharp black suit, when Trish grabs my elbow. The sudden touch makes me gasp and pull back until I see it's her. "It's just you," I say with my hand on my chest, catching my breath.

"Shit, sorry. I didn't mean to scare you," she tells me before looking left and right.

"Are you okay?" she asks me.

"I'm scared."

"Don't be. It's taken care of. Kam tied up the loose ends."

Shaking my head, I close my eyes and remind myself

we're standing in the middle of a crowded room. "But he knows. Zander ..."

"My brother trusts him. I trust him. You do too, right?"

My head shakes again as I try to explain, "I love him ... I'm worried that he ... he knows what I've done now."

"Oh," she says and breathes out, my concern finally getting through to her.

"He knows I'm ... that I've done things." I speak just lower than a murmur, just barely enough for her to hear, "Enough things that the sight of a dead body doesn't faze me."

Her lips turn down slightly before she decides to say, "Go find him. I bet the moment you two are alone, everything will be all right and you'll stop worrying."

She nods as she speaks, as if she's convinced herself as well.

"Thanks, I'll go do that."

"Let me know how it goes, all right?" she questions and I give her a quiet nod before continuing my way to the detail watching me.

"Silas, where's Zander?" I ask him.

"He'll be back in just a moment. How are you doing? Is there anything I can get you?" he asks.

"I'm just fine, and looking for a dance partner," I joke with Silas who somehow manages to look even more straitlaced than usual.

"I'm going to have to pass on that one," he answers with his hands raised. I let out a small laugh and leave Silas be in search for Zander. Plenty of time has passed and Kam knows he'll need to be seen soon. Or else everyone will know he was missing.

He stands with his hands clasped beside the hired security and no one would know he's only here for me.

Well ... it's possible someone could find out, but Kam would squash that from being released in a heartbeat. As far as social media is concerned, I'm back, in love and doing so much better.

Thanks to Charlie's exclusive and the snapshots taken only hours ago, the hashtags #SecondChanceInLove and #KnightInShiningArmor are trending all over the internet now.

No one is the wiser and they don't have to be.

The thing is, I don't know how to not be crazy.

For a moment I was with James because we ignored it all. Kam kept us safe in our little bubble. Well, it's more like *they* kept me safe in my little bubble.

Kam's killed for me. James killed for me. I don't want Zander to kill for me, but I think he would. No. I *know* he would. That doesn't matter, though, not right now. What matters is that I know I'd kill for him.

I think he might want to prove he can protect me here, but we have lived different lives and this world

... this world that reigns over me is manipulative and abusive. Its mercilessness is never ending.

And that is one thing Zander is not. He's too good for me. We both know it.

My only hope is that he takes me away. Somewhere off the grid where no one can reach us.

As I'm rounding the corner towards the bar for another snow ... whatever Trish called it, I spot him, like a beacon, standing tall and laughing at something said to him at the bar. A man in a suit stands next to him, laughing as well.

It seems casual. Small talk at the bar while waiting on drinks. He blends in so well. So easily and yet he's nothing like any of the men here. I'm caught in a trance when he turns, facing me, a drink in each hand and his gaze meets mine as if he knew I was watching all along.

As he smirks, heading toward me, I can't help but blush. Even if it's all an act.

There's a side of me that would stay just like this and deal with the hell that comes with this life, if he would pretend like nothing's changed.

But I know tonight has changed everything.

With that somber thought, he reaches me and hands me my drink. With one sip, I know it's the same one as before.

"Are we okay?" I ask him and to my surprise he tells

me, "I don't know how I'll be able to fool my brother. I think he'll suspect and I'm just hoping he doesn't ask."

It's all spoken under his breath and then he takes a swig of his drink.

I hesitate to clarify. "I mean us. Are we okay?" I gesture between us, feeling the nightlife fade to nothing as he stares back at me.

"We need to stay for at least another hour and when we get home, I'm going to punish you for doubting us." He leans forward as the heat rises between us and whispers in the crook of my neck, "From here on out, any question if we're all right will be met with my palm to your ass."

Chapter 20

Zander

I've lost track of time in the shower in Ella's house. The steam has surrounded me for what feels like forever. My thoughts keep distracting me.

There's a lot to process from the evening. A hell of a lot. I have some uncertainty about whether I'll be able to keep it a secret from Cade.

But no. Of course I will. That was the price, and it's worth every penny. I don't think he suspects anything just yet but when the reports come out that he's missing, I know he'll ask me. After all, I admitted I wanted that prick dead. Fuck. I brace my palms against the tiled wall and let the water come down on me.

He's my brother, they're my team. If they ask or push

for information, I'll ask them to look the other way. God knows I've done the same for each of them before. They owe me. They damn well know they do.

The bathroom door opens and Ella steps inside, bringing me from the menacing thoughts back to the present.

"Jailbird," I murmur so low I don't know if she even heard me. I can see her through the glass, though it's pretty well fogged up. I want this night washed off my skin.

"Can I come in with you?" she asks as the water beats down around me.

"Of course you can." I open the door for her and tell her, "Always."

She strips off her dress, letting the expensive silk pool around her feet and then her lace bra and panties come next. Her necklace stays on as she steps into the shower. That eases something in me. Something that feared this moment. The quiet car ride with Silas driving was difficult enough. Then I had to leave her to debrief. Now that the two of us are alone, it feels right again.

Her dark hair is wet almost immediately as she leans her head back, letting the spray hit her face. Her body trembles slightly and I hold her, pulling her back into my chest. With an arm around her waist, she clings to me. Her eyes are still closed. Ella seemed a lot more put together at the party, but now everything seems to be hitting her. That's to be expected.

"You did so well," I compliment her and kiss her temple. It's only a small sad smile that she gives me in return, her eyes still closed.

"Could you hold me for a while?" she asks.

"Yes." I pull her in tighter and love that she holds me back. "You held yourself together perfectly," I tell her.

"Did I?" she says with a little laugh. "I don't feel held together."

"Tell me how you're feeling," I say.

"I want to forget tonight."

"Is there anything I should be worried about?" I ask her.

She shakes her head against my chest. The water feels warm and cleansing. This transition is going to be difficult as hell, but the shower seems to be making it easier. "After this, we're leaving everything that happened tonight behind us."

"I hope so," she murmurs and that's not the answer I want to hear.

"Talk to me," I say and rock her slightly, giving her time to adjust and decompress.

"I'm scared," Ella admits and it's only then that her dark eyes open and stare ahead.

I almost tell her that we're going to be fine. That Kam has a strategy, and I'm going to follow it. That this is the life I'm choosing. I'm choosing her.

I have to think every sentence over before I can speak.

"We're going to be okay," I tell her, and I mean it. Fully. I'll sacrifice anything for her, which means we'll both be good.

"We are?" Ella looks up at me through her lashes.

"Yes, little bird. We are free of all of this shit after tomorrow."

Her gaze turns hopeful and then I tell her, "For the rest of our lives, we will be together and I will take care of you in every way possible."

She pulls me down to kiss her right there in the hot water. I feel all the tension go out of my muscles and then the rest of my body. I just want to feel surrounded by her. I'm taller than Ella but the heat of the shower helps. She kisses me slow from over her shoulder and then deeper until finally she moans into my mouth.

I want this with her always.

"I still need to spank your ass," I murmur against her lips as my hand slips to her front, down between her legs so I can rub her clit. "But I want you now and I'm going to fuck you so hard tonight you forget everything else other than what I do to you right now in this shower."

Her moan of approval is all I need to massage her breast, tugging her nipple and kissing her savagely. Every passing second getting hotter and heavier. I take her roughly, and her legs nearly give out as she comes.

I pick her up into my arms, spread her legs around my hips, and thrust inside her. Ella gasps. She grinds down onto my cock, her head pressed against the wall of the shower, her back braced in my arms, but then she slows the pace.

"I just want to look at you." She wraps her arms around my shoulders and holds on tight. The water splashes against my back as I kiss her once and then again.

"I don't know how long I can let you do that." I honestly don't. She feels so good wrapped around my cock. Leaning forward to kiss her again, I almost call her jailbird. But after tonight, I don't think I could ever call her that again. She's only my little bird now. Now and forevermore.

I peer down at her in my arms. Ella's hair is beautiful like this, with wet strands in her face. Her cheeks are rosy from the heat of the shower, and her body ... Well, I'll never want for anything with her.

"Tell me it's going to be okay?" she asks although it's spoken like a demand.

"There's nothing to worry about," I tell her, not because I'm trying to convince her. Because I believe it so strongly. We have nothing to worry about.

"I feel safe with you," she says and then a smile slips onto those gorgeous lips. "I guess that's always been true. Did you feel it too, even all the way back in that courtroom? That first day?"

It's true. "Yes," I say, then kiss her. "And that feeling is going to last until the end of our lives." I thrust up once and kiss the crook of her neck.

Ella grinds down onto me again arching her back, tipping her head back, and I let out a groan. "I'm going to come if you keep doing that."

My balls draw up and my toes curl from the pleasure that brings me right to the edge. I push her back against the shower and fuck her mercilessly.

Ella tips her head forward and looks into my eyes as she moans. There's no deeper connection than this. Her breathing quickens and she pleads my name in a way that makes me pause, buried deep inside of her.

"Are you okay?" I murmur, barely keeping my voice in check. My body shakes with the need to come but I won't do it until Ella comes too. "Is something wrong?"

"No," she gasps. "I'm just ... I love you, Z."

"I love you too." I kiss her deeply as I fuck her with a primitive need.

She comes with a gasp and a cry that turns into a moan. It's the most beautiful thing I've ever seen.

Chapter 21

Ella

A handful of months can make quite the difference. Crossing my ankles as I sit on the sofa in my blue room, I'm feeling especially thankful for the lit gas fireplace with its blue flames. Outside, snow is just starting to fall.

I remember the first time these men came into this room and took hold of my life. It feels like a lifetime ago. Here we are in nearly the same positions, but everything has changed.

"There we are," Kam states firmly, clicking the end of the pen and handing the signed paper to Cade who checks it over and then signs himself.

"Is that the last of them?" Z asks from my right,

an arm around my shoulders possessively. I lean into him and rest my head on his shoulder. I could hardly sleep last night and I know the moment the papers are scanned and filed and everyone leaves this room, I'm going to sleep soundly.

"It's the last of what he wanted to see, yes."

"There won't even be a hearing?" I question.

"Not in person," Kam tells me. "The judge said that with everyone in agreement it's as simple as dotting the I's and crossing the T's."

I don't dare smile, although one begs to appear as Z kisses my temple.

"I would say get a room, but we all know you two consider the entire house your room," Cade mutters as he stacks the papers and taps them on the coffee table to organize them neatly.

His comment forces me to smirk and the other men chuckle lightly. I bury my hands in my oversized cream sweater and bring my knees up to my chest. All the while, leaning against Z.

"If you're ever not okay, you know you can call me," Damon says from where he stands to the right of the fireplace.

"Me too," Cade says and I'm caught off guard. I look up at him, hoping there's never a reason we would need The Firm. "He can be an ass sometimes. You can call me, I'll kick his ass for you," he jokes.

A laugh bubbles up but it's muted. I appreciate the lightheartedness but it just hasn't hit home yet.

"You're tense, Ella. Loosen up, babe. You're free today. Now you could tell me to get out and I'd actually have to listen." Kam smiles a boyish grin. "Not that I'm going to listen, but you could do it."

At that Zander laughs a deep, rough chuckle that shakes me gently.

"I'll keep that in mind," I comment back.

"Let's give these two a moment," Kam suggests to the room.

Cade and Kam lead the men out to the kitchen and I watch them go. It won't be the last time they're here. As much as Zander is a part of my life, I'm a part of The Firm's life. Even if Z has decided to take a leave of absence for an indefinite amount of time.

He and his brother decided it would be best for him to take time off for this transition. Mostly because I asked him to. I am his greedy selfish girl, after all.

The moment the room is quiet and the men's conversation can barely be heard, Z turns me in his arms so I'm facing him. His black tee clings to his broad shoulders and his rough stubble is a bit more than a five o'clock shadow. His smile is easy and charming as if there's nothing to worry about any longer.

"He said I need to marry you," Z says far too calmly.

"What?" I can't hide the shock in my voice. "Kam said that?"

He only nods as I stare at him wide eyed.

"When I ask you to marry me, it will be because I want you to be my wife," he tells me with certainty as he slips down off the sofa.

My heart races as I stare into his hazel eyes flecked with gold. His necklace is still where it will always be. "You gave me a ring already," I whisper, my fingers fiddling with the rose gold ring through the sweater.

He smirks, pulling a ring from his back pocket and says, "I can give you more than one, can't I?"

My bottom lip drops at the sight of the oval diamond. It's surrounded by small black diamonds all the way around. My hand trembles as I reach out to take it.

"You have to say you'll marry me first," Z says, staring back at me with a devilish grin.

The moment I kiss him, a hand on each side of his face, a champagne bottle pops and applause fills the room.

With tears pricking the back of my eyes, I look to my left and see them all standing in the doorway, watching with genuine happiness for the two of us.

"Let her say yes first," Z manages to get out.

"Yes." I'm quick to answer. "Yes a million times, yes."

Chapter 22

Zander

Two months later

Outside the doors to the courtroom, I take Ella's hand in mine. These aren't the same doors I stood behind six months ago when I first laid eyes on her, but the dark grooved floor-to-ceiling doors are reminiscent of how we started.

She's dressed in a long white lace dress and I'm wearing a gray suit she picked out. The same suit I wear for court appearances. Funny, because this is one of sorts I suppose.

With a simper on her bloodred lips and a dark curl loose from her bun, she looks up at me. Nothing but happiness shines back in her chestnut eyes. My little bird looks stunning, actually. She had her stylist come over and do her makeup and her hair for the ceremony.

She planned every detail of today. It's amazing how quickly a girl can pull together a wedding.

It's nothing big like I thought she might want. There's no fancy ceremony in a tall cathedral. There's no press. And the reception is more like a laid-back after-party. No, this isn't the big deal I want to give Ella, but we can always do that later. Having a life together ... that's the biggest deal of all.

"Are you ready?" I ask her, giving her hand a squeeze. She squeezes back and lets out a breath while giving me an uncontained, confident smile.

"Yes. I'm more than ready to be your wife, Mr. Thompson."

Cade claps his hand on my shoulder just then and I had nearly forgot he was there. "Let's head in?" he asks.

I smirk down at my soon-to-be wife and say, "Let's."

"We're next on the list," Cade tells me and I have to hold back my huff of impatience. It's not the sexiest part of a courthouse wedding. We had to wait for another couple in front of us, and then for the judge to rule on a traffic violation.

The man who got the ticket didn't have to pay his fine after all. The judge has been finishing up with him. He comes out the right door as my brother pulls open the left.

"Congratulations," he says, his face happy and bright. Our attire is the opposite of his jeans and leather jacket. Even without a veil or bouquet, I'm certain it's obvious what we're here for. I happily accept his good wishes.

"Thank you," Ella and I answer in unison and in this moment, I couldn't feel lighter or happier or like this moment was meant to be.

Our footsteps in sync with one another, we go into the courtroom together. Ella and I go down the aisle with my brother, Damon on my side and Trish and Kam on hers. My heart races as we take our places in front of the judge.

It's the exact opposite of how it was when things started. Ella was sitting up at that table with the lawyers. I was sitting in the back, wondering how a woman like her ever came to be in that position. I'd wanted to know everything about her.

Now I get to spend the rest of my life learning all the details I could ever hope to learn.

"Your paperwork?" The judge, an old man, smiles at us. I pass over the marriage license and he scans it as if it's the most important document of the day. "Witnesses?" he asks next.

My brother steps up. So does Trish.

The judge welcomes them, then comes down and takes his place in front of us. "Marriage is a civil union," he begins. "It's about two people coming together. And in spite of great odds."

Ella glances at me, uncontained joy on her face.

"We know that life can deal us some blows," the judge says. "Can put us through the wringer. But what I like best about weddings is that they're all about hope. All of them, every single one, is about hope. Take the bride's hands in yours," he tells me.

Without a second thought, I do what he says. I take Ella's hands in mine. I was already holding one of her hands. Now I have them both, clasped in mine. When she looks at me again her eyes are shining.

Hope. This wedding is about hope. That we're going to have our happily ever after together, an ending neither of us saw coming.

"Zander Thompson," the judge says. "Do you take this woman to be your lawfully wedded wife, in the eyes of God, in the state of Pennsylvania?"

"I do," I say.

"And Eleanor Bordeu," he says, "do you take this man to be your lawfully wedded husband, in the eyes of God, in the state of Pennsylvania?"

"I do," she whispers.

"The rings," the judge says. Cade steps forward with

my ring for Ella. "Place the ring on her ring finger."

I do. Ella blinks down at it like it's worth more than all the money she had in her past. "This is a symbol of my love for you," I tell her. "I love you."

Ella repeats this process with my ring, only she's breathing harder. Tears escape from the corner of her eyes. "None of that, you'll ruin that dress with mascara," Kam jokingly whispers and Ella lets out a small laugh.

"This is a symbol of my love for you. I love you."

I miss a few sentences of the ceremony because I'm staring into her eyes.

"... vested in me by the state of Pennsylvania, you may kiss your bride," the judge announces.

I lean in and kiss Ella. My brother cheers. It's too loud for the courtroom, but it doesn't matter. Everybody's clapping. Our friends. Members of The Firm. It's a small wedding, a tiny wedding party, and the reception will be just as small, but I don't care.

We file out of the courtroom, our friends offering congratulations. A local photographer snaps photos of us outside the courthouse, all of us in different configurations. As the final photos are taken, my brother slaps me on the back.

"To the restaurant we go?" I question, not sure if she wants to take more photos or not. She said she wanted laid back, but with her, I'm not exactly sure she knows how to do "laid back."

Ella smiles up at me, a knowing look in her eyes. "I thought we could stop by the new place first. I ... I have a second dress to change into."

Trish laughs beside us. "Color me surprised," she jokes and rubs her elbow against Ella's. "Small wedding, but big fashion."

Cade looks to her, then back at me. "So you two closed on the new place?"

"We signed on the dotted line more than once today," I tell him. We couldn't have done it without Kam.

Cade nods, smiling. "Were you happy with the ceremony, Ella?"

She nods eagerly. "I'm even more excited for the reception. We'll only be a few minutes behind you guys."

"I guess it's too late to tell you," Cade says, pretending to look worried.

"Tell me what?"

"That I'm not sure you've thought enough about marrying Zander. You might change your mind."

"Never," Ella says, laughing.

"We just need to pick up our new house keys. Then we'll meet you at the restaurant."

All of our friends agree with us. They're all so happy to be here. This is what it must feel like to start over.

"Don't take too long," Cade admonishes.

"You'd better not lose track of time," Trish says with a mock scowl. "Ella, I want to dance with you on your wedding day."

Kam comments dryly, "Don't let Zander keep you in that house all night."

"I won't. I promise," Ella tells them.

"Half an hour?" Trish says. "Forty-five minutes?"

"Half an hour," I tell her. Then I take Ella's hand in mine and lead her away from the people we love.

"Thirty minutes isn't a long time," she murmurs.

"All we have to do is pick up the keys."

"That's all?" Ella asks, her tone low and sensual.

"I can do a lot in thirty minutes, little bird. But we have a reception to get to. Then forever is waiting for us."

Epilogue

Zander

One year later …

Ella leans over the bed, beautiful and very pregnant. This is just about the only way we can have sex now that she's in her third trimester. Her hands on pillows, me behind her.

Naked with her thick dark hair thrown over her shoulder, she peeks back behind me and lets out the sweetest, sexiest moan I've ever heard.

I sink into her again and again, slowly. It's past the point where we can have the rough, intense sex we used to have. She craves something different now. She still loves it when I pay extra attention to her clit, though.

It's apparently more sensitive now.

But she's still mine in every way, so I put my hand around her throat just for the pressure and slow the pace even more. Her lips form a perfect O.

She feels like fucking heaven like this. Everything about her makes me crave more and more of her.

I want to feel her come around me, and she's hot and tight, even more so in her pregnancy. She pants as she gets close, then comes, throwing her head back in pure delight. It's a slow orgasm that seems to go on and on and on. The way her warmth strokes my cock nearly brings me to the edge with her. I linger in her new slickness.

I will never have enough of her.

I let my hands roam down her curves and I lose control, just a little, and pump into her harder. Ella braces against the bed and takes it. Her fingers curl over the covers, gripping them as she lets out a strangled groan. That sound is what does it for me, and I lose myself in her. She's so good for me. She always is.

Afterward, she turns just enough to kiss me. A quick peck before lying down and waiting for me to clean her up.

"Come," I command her and she protests with the smallest sound of resistance, snuggling into the sheets. "I want to shower with you," I bend down to tell her and nip her earlobe.

It only takes nudging her nose with mine for her to agree and the two of us make our way into the shower. It's all tiled in an antique blue, with top-of-the-line furnishings. Ella picked out every piece from the art on the wall, to the extra-large linen closets.

Even the shower is oversized so we could do just this.

Our house is the same way. A new build, out by the beach and as I turn the faucet on, the salty breeze blows in through the open window. We're not very close to the neighbors, which is how I like it. Ella too. We don't have to worry about photographers out here. There isn't a soul for a good half mile in any direction.

All I have to worry about is making sure she's rubbed down to her satisfaction under the hot water.

I marvel at her new shape. It's something else, seeing her grow so beautifully. Our baby will be born this year, almost two years after we first met. This last year has been nothing but calm, with me devoted to her and her devoted to me.

We'll bring that child here, to our house. I'll be able to take him or her on walks on warm mornings.

It'll be peaceful.

That's all I can ask for, really.

I take my time caring for her. Washing her body and kissing as I go. She does this little hum I love all the while. Her eyes close and I know she's going to nap after this.

For me, I'll be monitoring what my brother emailed yesterday. A new case that he wants my opinion on.

"All done, you can leave me now and sleep," I say and tease her with a kiss on her shoulder.

"Mmm, you don't want to nap with me?" she offers and almost any other day I would at least lie down with her. "Not today, little bird."

Ella leans against me, warm and satisfied but with a pout that tells me she may push me, just to. That mouth of hers hasn't changed. It appears she's too tired for that. I help her out of the shower and she gathers a towel around her.

When we've finished with our shower and I've put the bathrobe over her shoulders, she tells me she wants to look over the nursery one more time today. I can only smirk and follow my wife to the room we've been in three times already today. It's directly next to the suite.

"I can't believe it's done," she remarks from the doorway.

"The baby's going to love it," I say.

"What about you?" she questions. "You'll probably spend a fair amount time in here too. I did choose the perfect glider."

"Of course you did, little bird. You choose all the perfect things."

"I love it here," Ella murmurs softly. It's a good thing.

She's spent hours decorating the nursery, making sure each detail is perfect. And a small fortune. Kam is still in charge of the funds, though, and according to him, she is set for life and can spend multiple small fortunes. The two of them ganged up on me to let her have the nursery she wanted. After all, this baby will be our first and only.

Down below on the street, a car moves down the road. In front of our house, the driver brakes and pulls the car to the curb.

"Oh," Ella says. "I'm not dressed...and that's Damon's car."

I almost disagree with her, saying it's just the same car as Damon's, not actually his. He doesn't have any reason to be here right now.

But then he steps out of the car, slams the door behind him, and jogs toward us. He barely glances around him, totally focused on getting to the house. The doorbell will ring any second.

"Get dressed." I press a kiss to Ella's forehead. "Looks like something's going on."

I don't tell her my brother said yesterday there may be trouble. I don't tell her he said something happened between a client and someone on the team. I barely skimmed his email; I haven't even opened the documents yet. But given that Damon's here ... I'm guessing he did something he shouldn't have.

The National Suicide Prevention Lifeline is a United States-based suicide prevention network of over 160 crisis centers that provides 24/7 service via a toll-free hotline at the number 1-800-273-8255. It is available to anyone in suicidal crisis or emotional distress.

About the Authors

Willow Winters

Thank you so much for reading my romances. I'm just a stay at home Mom and an avid reader turned Author and I couldn't be happier.

I hope you love my books as much as I do!

More by Willow Winters
www.willowwinterswrites.com/books

Amelia Wilde

USA today bestselling author of dangerous contemporary romance and loves it a little too much. She lives in Michigan with her husband and daughters. She spends most of her time typing furiously on an iPad and appreciating the natural splendor of her home state from where she likes it best: inside.

More by Amelia Wilde
www.awilderomance.com/

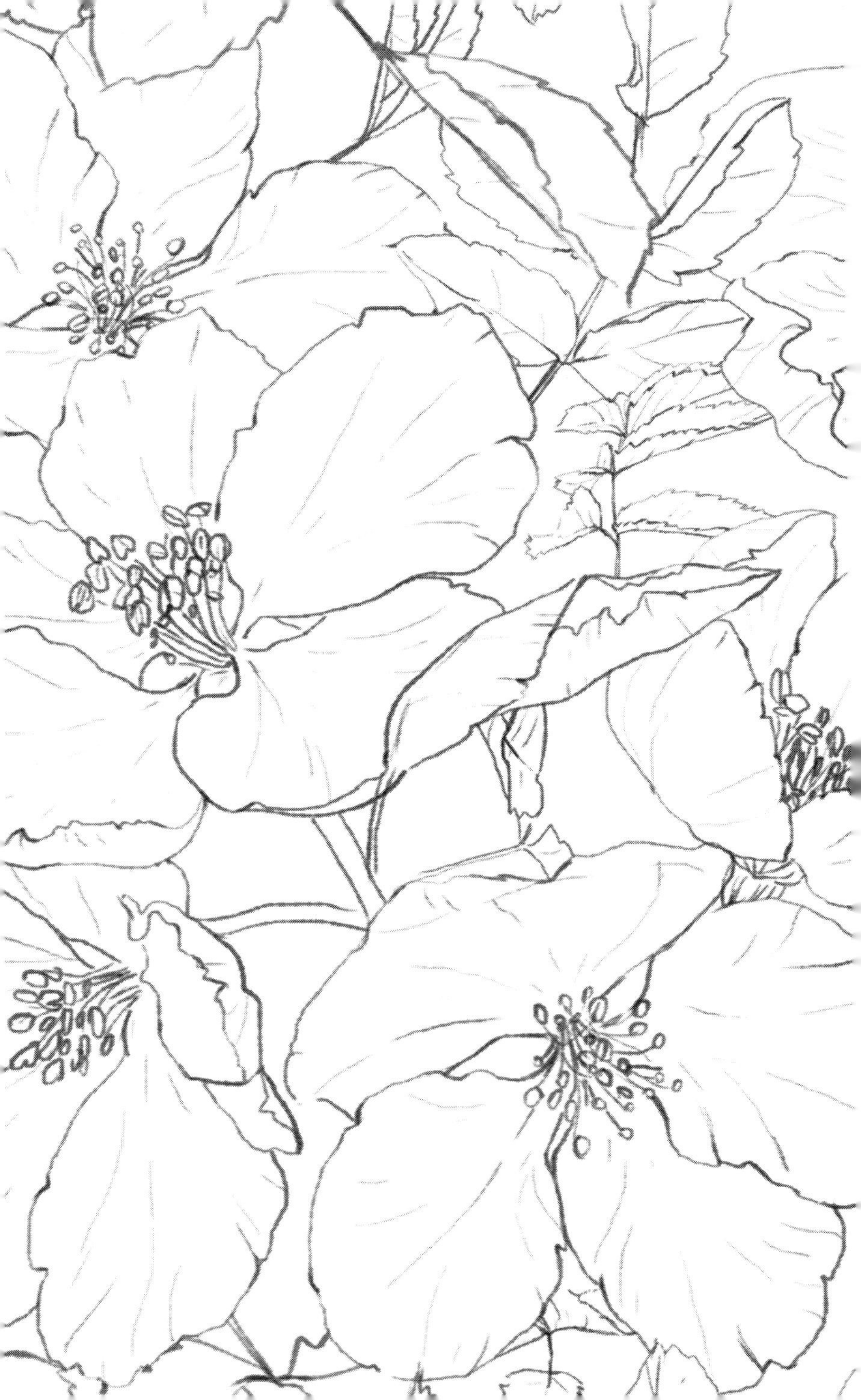

Printed in Great Britain
by Amazon